CHRISTMAS BY THE BAY

BLUE HERON COTTAGES
BOOK SEVEN

KAY CORRELL

ZURA LU PUBLISHING LLC

This book is dedicated to the wonderful holidays I've celebrated in my life through the years. To the many Christmas ornaments I've collected over the years and the memories they bring. To the wonderful recipes passed down in our family for generations. To the family who surrounds us this holiday season and the ones we are dearly missing.

May your holiday season be filled with love and joy.

Christmas by the Bay

Violet is all about the holiday season this year —
her first one as owner of Blue Heron Cottages.
But what she isn't expecting for Christmas is
meeting Danny Parker - no relation to the
Moonbeam Parkers. Danny and his daughter
come to stay at the cottages for the holidays and
his daughter is not pleased. At all.

Rose returns to the cottages to be surrounded by
friends, but her heart aches as she prepares to
spend her first Christmas without her beloved
Emmett.

Aspen is sure Walker is hiding something. Or maybe he's losing interest in her... Then, to make things worse, her sister cancels plans to come to the cottages for Christmas.

Can Moonbeam and the Blue Heron Cottages weave their magic and provide the perfect Christmas for everyone?

Continue on with the Blue Heron Cottages series, a touching saga of love, resilience, and the profound connections we stumble upon in the unlikeliest of places. It's a journey through love, loss, and ultimately, the transformative power of friendship.

KAY'S BOOKS

Find more information on all my books at
kaycorrell.com
Buy direct from Kay's Shop at
shop.kaycorrell.com

COMFORT CROSSING ~ THE SERIES
The Shop on Main - Book One
The Memory Box - Book Two
The Christmas Cottage - A Holiday Novella
(Book 2.5)
The Letter - Book Three
The Christmas Scarf - A Holiday Novella
(Book 3.5)
The Magnolia Cafe - Book Four
The Unexpected Wedding - Book Five

The Wedding in the Grove - (a crossover short story between series - with Josephine and Paul from The Letter.)

LIGHTHOUSE POINT ~ THE SERIES
Wish Upon a Shell - Book One
Wedding on the Beach - Book Two
Love at the Lighthouse - Book Three
Cottage near the Point - Book Four
Return to the Island - Book Five
Bungalow by the Bay - Book Six
Christmas Comes to Lighthouse Point - Book Seven

CHARMING INN ~ Return to Lighthouse Point
One Simple Wish - Book One
Two of a Kind - Book Two
Three Little Things - Book Three
Four Short Weeks - Book Four
Five Years or So - Book Five
Six Hours Away - Book Six
Charming Christmas - Book Seven

SWEET RIVER ~ THE SERIES
A Dream to Believe in - Book One
A Memory to Cherish - Book Two

A Song to Remember - Book Three
A Time to Forgive - Book Four
A Summer of Secrets - Book Five
A Moment in the Moonlight - Book Six

MOONBEAM BAY ~ THE SERIES

The Parker Women - Book One
The Parker Cafe - Book Two
A Heather Parker Original - Book Three
The Parker Family Secret - Book Four
Grace Parker's Peach Pie - Book Five
The Perks of Being a Parker - Book Six

BLUE HERON COTTAGES ~ THE SERIES

Memories of the Beach - Book One
Walks along the Shore - Book Two
Bookshop near the Coast - Book Three
Restaurant on the Wharf - Book Four
Lilacs by the Sea - Book Five
Flower Shop on Magnolia - Book Six
Christmas by the Bay - Book Seven
Plus more to come!

WIND CHIME BEACH ~ A stand-alone novel

INDIGO BAY ~

Sweet Days by the Bay - Kay's Complete
Collection of stories in the Indigo Bay series

Sign up for my newsletter at my website
kaycorrell.com to make sure you don't miss any
new releases or sales.

PROLOGUE

R ose stood on the steps to her house, her heart stumbling as she shakily held out the key. It took three tries to get the key settled into the lock and turn it. She swung the door open and stepped inside, bracing herself against the wave of emotions rising up and threatening to smother her.

One deep breath and she set the keys down on the table by the door. The memories swirled around her. She swept her gaze around the room.

The late afternoon sun filtered in through the windows, bathing the worn leather couch that Emmett had loved so much. An old pair of his shoes still peeked out from beneath the couch. He never seemed to remember to put them away, but she hadn't really minded. She'd just always gone behind him and put them away in their closet.

Why had she left those shoes there for so many months? That was silly, wasn't it? But somehow, putting them away—or worse yet, packing them up—seemed so final.

She straightened her shoulders. But that was exactly why she was back here. Someone could make good use of his clothes if she donated them. It was silly and selfish to just let them hang in the closet.

She walked over to the couch and ran her hand along the arm, the leather soft to her touch. She closed her eyes, imagining Emmett sitting there. Reading a book. Watching television. Or just sitting there talking to her.

Opening her eyes, she headed to the kitchen and got a drink of water from the faucet, glancing out the back window at the garden. What was left of the garden in late fall, anyway.

She'd have to go out there and clean it up. After setting the glass in the sink, she went over to the fridge and tugged the door open, then shook her head. She hadn't planned on staying so long in Moonbeam. The original plan had been to stay for one week. But one week became two, which became a month, which became longer…

But she finally knew she had to return home. There were decisions to be made. Things to be done.

Starting with cleaning out the fridge and throwing out the expired items. She grabbed the trash bin and started to work. It was easier to face throwing away the food than think about packing up Emmett's things.

She wasn't sure how she was going to get through all of this. She didn't really want help with it though. It was something she needed to do. Say goodbye to his things. Let them go. No matter how hard it was going to be.

After finishing with the fridge, she decided the kitchen needed a good cleaning. It was evening by the time she was done. She should have gone by the grocery store for something to make for dinner. Staring into the pantry, she spotted a packet of microwave popcorn. That would work. She popped the corn and poured herself a glass of wine. Her favorite wrap was hanging by the back door, and she draped it over her shoulders.

She headed out to the back porch and sat down with her bowl of popcorn and glass of wine. She used to love to sit out here with Emmett. They'd come out and talk about their days. Unwind. Watch the birds at the bird feeder. Not that there were any birds at the feeder now. The seed was long gone since she'd been away in Moonbeam for so long.

She gently rocked back and forth, watching the evening darken and the night appear with its sparkling stars dotting the sky. Emmett knew all of the constellations, and she tried to recall their names as she stared up at the sky. Why hadn't she memorized them when she had the chance?

"Emmett, I miss you so much," she whispered into the darkness. "I have some hard decisions to make. I just need to get up my courage to make them."

Long after the popcorn and wine were gone, she remained sitting there, her wrap—the one Emmett had bought her—comforting her as she rocked back and forth, as if he had his arm around her.

She finally stood and brought her dishes inside, setting them in the sink. Then she turned out the light and headed down the long hall to their bedroom. *Her* bedroom.

Tears slowly rolled down her cheeks as she sat on the bed. It was so hard being back here.

And yet, how could she bear to give up the home they'd shared for so many years?

But how could she move on with her life if she stayed? And Emmett would want her to move on. He'd said so in the long days of his illness when she'd sat by his bedside. And she'd promised him she would.

But it was so hard to actually keep that promise...

CHAPTER 1

W EEKS LATER...

Violet stood back, eyeing the Christmas tree she'd just put up in the reception area of Blue Heron Cottages. Was it crooked? She tilted her head. Yes, it definitely leaned to the left. And just a minute ago, it leaned to the right. Annoyed, she stood with her hands on her hips, inspecting the tree that wouldn't cooperate. Then she crawled back under the tree once again.

The door opened and her brother came in. "Oh, hey. You got the tree up." Rob narrowed his eyes. "But it's crooked."

7

"Thanks. I always love hearing your opinion." Her words came out a bit sharper than she intended. She stood up, took a step back, and let out a long sigh. "I know it. I keep adjusting it but then it tilts in the other direction."

"Here, let me help."

Even though she hated that Rob was always rescuing her, she could use the help. He stepped closer, grabbed the trunk, and adjusted it, shoving it farther down into the stand.

And the tree stood perfectly straight. Of course.

He grinned in triumph with a flourish of his hand. "Ta-da."

She glared at the tree. One move from Rob and it decided to behave? She hated having Rob fix things for her. Things she should be able to do herself. She gave him a weak smile. "Yes, thanks."

"It's a bit early to put up a tree, don't you think?"

"And thanks for that opinion, too." She turned and headed behind the reception desk.

"Hey, I'm sorry." Rob crossed over. "I know you're excited about the holidays this year. I am too. Should be fun to spend them with Evelyn and her family."

Rob had married into a big family this year, but it left her feeling just a bit left out. She'd thought it would be just Rob and her this Christmas. Until he fell in love with Evelyn and married her. But her brother was happy, so that's what mattered.

"You want me to put the lights on the tree?" he offered.

"I haven't gone through all the boxes of decorations in the storeroom yet. I'll put them up soon."

"You need any help with anything else?"

"No, I've got everything covered." Why did he always think she needed help? She was doing a fine job of running the resort. Well, pretty fine. A little mix-up here and there, like when she double booked a cottage last week. Or forgot to order more cleaning supplies. But all in all, she was proud of how she was doing with the resort. Especially after Rob had been so disapproving of her decision to buy it. At least he had been at first. Now he seemed more used to the idea. Probably because he'd settled down here in Moonbeam with Evelyn.

"You don't call me to come over and fix

things very often." He straightened a stack of papers on the reception desk.

"You're busy. You have your books to write and a wife now and..." She shrugged. "I'm doing okay. And I found a handyman to call if I need him."

"You can always call me." Rob looked the tiniest bit hurt.

"I know. I just——"

"Want to do it on your own." He smiled. "I get that. But the offer stands. Always willing to help."

"Thanks, Robbie." He really was a great brother. Even if he did have way too many opinions that he offered up at every moment.

"Okay, well I'm off. I'm going to try and finish my book today. The ending is fighting me."

"I thought the beginning of books fought you?"

"Yes, that too. What can I say?" He laughed. "Anyway, planning on being here for happy hour on Friday. Evelyn will try to make it too."

"Great, hope to see both of you then."

Her Friday night happy hours had become quite the gathering here in town. Not only the guests, but her friends from town came too. It was nice to start feeling like she belonged here in Moonbeam.

Rob waved as he walked out the door. She immediately spread out the pages he'd straightened—they were fine the way they had been in a slightly messy stack—and turned to the computer and frowned. Rob had gotten her all set up on a hospitality software program. Yet another time he'd stepped in to help. More like insisted because her bookkeeping skills kept falling apart before he installed the software. She had to admit it did make part of the job easier, but she still had to keep looking things up and figuring out how to do things with the program.

The tree caught her attention again, and she'd swear it was begging her for lights. She'd have to find time to dig in the storage room and see what decorations had been left there. She couldn't wait to get the reception area all decorated for Christmas.

"I'm not going." Allison planted her hands on her hips and glared at him. Danny closed his eyes and counted to ten. When he opened them, his daughter was still standing there with her chin jutting out defiantly.

"Allison, you don't have a choice. We're getting away through the holidays. I booked us a cottage at the beach in a place called Moonbeam."

"I'm not leaving my friends."

"You're grounded, so you wouldn't be seeing them anyway."

"You can't keep me from seeing them. It's almost Christmas. There are so many parties and stuff."

"None of which you'll be going to. You do understand there are consequences to your actions, right? You were suspended from school until classes resume in January. That's serious, Allison. You need to straighten up and figure things out. With the antics you're pulling and failing grades, you'll never get into college."

"Who says I want to go to college?" Her blue eyes flashed at him and she looked remarkably like her mother when Linda tried to get her way.

"You should at least leave your options open." How many times had they had this same conversation?

"I'll just go live with Mom. She won't make me leave."

A long, tired sigh escaped him. Sometimes it seemed like it would be easier to just let her go live with Linda. But that wouldn't be the best thing for Allison. Linda was a lousy mother. She couldn't be bothered with actually taking care of her daughter and had left when Allison was just five years old. Said it was all just too much for her. She needed her space.

Her space included a long line of boyfriends even before he'd finally filed for divorce. Linda would disappear for months on end. Come back to visit for a bit. Then things would settle down and almost be normal. But then she'd leave again, often without saying goodbye to Allison. No wonder his daughter acted out.

But she was getting older now. Sixteen. She needed to realize that actions have consequences.

And she needed a new group of friends. They'd moved from Atlanta to Tallahassee a few years back when he took a new job. It had taken Alli a while to make friends. At first, he was just pleased she had friends. But then she dropped out of sports, choir, and all after-school activities. Started getting into trouble at school and not doing her classwork.

And now she was *suspended*. He still couldn't quite wrap his head around that.

"I'm going to go call Mom right now. I'm sure she'll come get me. She won't make me leave. I'd rather live with her, anyway."

Ouch. He knew she was just reacting to his decision that they go away, but it still hurt. He'd been her only parent, for all intents and purposes, her whole life. Always been there for her.

Allison flounced out of the room, stomped down the hall, and slammed the door to her bedroom.

He sank onto a kitchen chair. It creaked under his weight. He kept meaning to get out some glue and fix it because the creaking annoyed him, but he'd been too busy to actually fix it.

He rested his forehead in his hands. No one had prepared him for this stage of life, raising a teenager. Not when they'd put that tiny baby girl in his arms and he'd fallen hopelessly in love with her. At the time, he thought endless nights of no sleep were the biggest problem. He'd give anything to go back to those days. Or the days when she was a toddler, waddling around, hanging onto his finger as she explored the world.

The last year or so had been so hard. And he no longer had his mother to depend on for backup. Her death had left a gaping hole in his life. In Allison's life. Life threatened to overwhelm him, but he fought it off. He didn't have time for that. He was the only adult Allison had to depend on no matter how tough things got. He was determined to be there for her. Even if he had to make tough decisions and enforce his choices, even when she rebelled.

He heard Allison's raised voice but couldn't quite make out the words. He was pretty sure he knew what was going on. Linda was telling her that she couldn't come stay with her. Linda had a brand-new boyfriend now, one she called her fiancé. But then, she'd had a lot of men she called that since they'd divorced, and only one had panned out and become a husband. That marriage had lasted six weeks.

He pushed himself off the chair—which annoyingly creaked again—and headed down the hallway. The sound of sobs filtered through Allison's door, and his heart clutched in his chest. Linda always fell short of being the mother Allison needed.

He knocked on her door. "Allison?"

"Go away."

"Allison, let's talk."

The door popped open and Allison stood there, her eyes puffy and swollen. "There's nothing to talk about unless it's to say we're not going to this stupid Moonbeam place."

"We are going."

"Mom said she's going out of town, so I can't stay with her."

"I see." He doubted that was the truth, but it probably hurt less for Allison to believe it.

"Can't we please stay here?" Her eyes begged him.

"No, we can't. We're going away for a few weeks. And you'll be doing your assignments remotely. Catching up on every single assignment you've missed this semester."

"But Dad—"

"Allison, you were drunk at school. Drunk." He still couldn't believe it. Why hadn't he realized the trouble she was getting into? "And we won't even get into the discussion about how underage you are. Alcohol is just not allowed. Do you understand me?"

"It was just that one time." She ducked her head away slightly, and he knew she was lying.

"I'm so disappointed in you, Allison. You're making poor choices."

"Sure, both my parents hate me. That's just great. Neither one of you wants me."

He reached out and touched her arm. "Ah, Allison. I love you more than anyone or anything in the whole world. You know that. I know you're mad now. But this trip is for the best. We need to get away. Change things."

"But—"

He held up his hand. "No, don't argue. This is just how it is. Be packed and ready to go first thing in the morning."

He turned, headed to his bedroom, and pulled a suitcase from the closet. He tossed it on the bed, then sank down beside it. Fatherhood was not for the weak, that was for sure.

But he was certain he was making the right decision. Get Allison away from the crowd she'd been running with. Make her take responsibility for her actions. Not make excuses for her or make it easier on her. She was getting older. Now was the time for some hard life lessons.

If it didn't kill him first…

CHAPTER 2

T he next day Violet searched and found a few boxes of bedraggled-looking Christmas decorations in the storage room of Blue Heron Cottages and carried them out to the reception area to sort through. She couldn't wait to get the office all decorated for the holidays. She was probably rushing the season, but it was her first Christmas here in Moonbeam and she couldn't wait to enjoy every single minute of it.

She grabbed one box and pulled out a tangle of twinkle lights. Before going to the effort to untangle them, she plugged in each strand. Not one of them worked. The wiring on them didn't look very safe, either. Okay, new lights.

Another box was full of broken ornaments and an old bunch of tinsel in a massive tangle. So far, she wasn't having much luck. Unfortunately, most of it just needed to be pitched. She'd have to go to Parker's General Store and get new decorations.

But that sounded kind of fun to her. She could pick out exactly what she wanted. She wanted lights in all the windows and decorations scattered all through the area. The tree with an angel on top. Imagining the room all decorated for the season brought a smile to her face. Rob would probably tell her she went overboard, but she didn't care.

She glanced out the window, and a man pulled up in a pickup truck. He stepped out and stretched. A girl got out from the passenger side. Must be the guests for the pink cottage. The man motioned for the girl to follow him, but she just stood by the truck and scowled. He shook his head, turned, and walked into the office.

"Good afternoon." She smiled at him. "Welcome to Blue Heron Cottages."

"Hi. I have a reservation. Danny Parker."

"Any relation to the Parkers here in Moonbeam?"

"Doubt it. My family is from Minnesota. Pretty common name."

She nodded. "So, reservation for two?"

"Yes, I'm here with my not-very-happy daughter." He shrugged. "My darling little girl turned into a teenager and it seems I don't do anything right. Especially planning this trip here and staying through the holidays. She acts like coming here to the beach is the worst punishment ever."

"I bet she'll warm up to the idea. There's lots to do here. And the beach is wonderful."

"I hope so. Otherwise, it's going to be a long few weeks."

Violet would have to agree with that sentiment if the girl, still standing outside with her arms crossed and the scowl etched firmly on her features, didn't change her attitude a little bit. "Here are your keys, Mr. Parker."

"Danny. Please call me Danny."

"Danny it is. And I'm Violet. I own Blue Heron Cottages."

"Nice to meet you." He smiled, but it didn't quite reach his eyes.

He stood tall, probably a good five inches taller than she was. He had a touch of gray at his temples, but she couldn't really guess his age. She was horrible at that.

"You're in the pink cottage. Right across the courtyard. Let me know if you need anything."

"Thank you." He took the keys, and she'd swear he squared his shoulders, gathering courage to go out and see his daughter again.

"Oh, and Mr. Park—Danny. On Fridays, I have a happy hour for all the guests in the courtyard. There's soda for the kids. And we have appetizers. Lots of them. I always seem to overdo it a bit. You should come tonight."

"I just might do that. Thanks." With that, he strode out the door looking like he was off to face a firing squad. Poor guy. Maybe his daughter would lighten up a bit when she found out how wonderful Moonbeam was.

Or not.

Violet was certainly no expert on teenage girls.

Aspen paused on her way to the office of Blue Heron Cottages and took the offered mail from the mail carrier. "Thanks, Hank. Have a good day."

"Have a good one, Aspen." He headed back down the walkway.

Who knew she'd ever live in a small town where she knew the mailman's first name and he knew hers? She adored living in Moonbeam. Humming softly, she sorted through the mail as she walked inside.

"Oh, look, another card from Rose. I love that she sends cards instead of emails or texts." Aspen walked up to the reception desk and handed the envelope to Violet.

"I love it too. It's just so… personal." Violet opened the envelope, pulled out the card, and laughed. She showed the front of the card to Aspen.

The card had an illustration of violets. So like Rose to pick a card like that. Violets for Violet.

Violet quickly read the note, then looked up. "She sounds like she's been busy. I can't believe it's already been over a month since she left."

"She is still planning on coming back for Christmas, isn't she?"

"She is. In just a few more days."

Aspen came behind the reception desk. "I saw a man and a girl heading into the pink cottage as I was coming in."

"Yes, they're here through Christmas. And I just got another reservation for Christmas week. That means we're completely booked for the holidays."

"Oh, that's great."

"And we have the cottage booked for your sister, and her family. I put them in the yellow cottage. Same one Willow stayed in before."

"She'll love that. I can't wait to see them again." Excitement and anticipation ran through her. "A real family gathering for Christmas. I've never had that before."

"I feel the same way. Rob would sometimes manage to visit during the holidays. But now we both live in the same town. It will be nice to spend Christmas with him and Evelyn."

"That's nice."

"I just have to figure out how to let you and me have our Christmas and still juggle running the resort."

"Maybe we could put a sign up that the office will be closed on Christmas Day? But leave a phone number in case an emergency comes up?" Aspen suggested.

"That's not a bad idea." Violet nodded. "We'll figure it out. And I want you to have lots of time with Walker and his family, as well as your sister."

"It's going to be the best Christmas." Aspen felt like a little girl waiting for Christmas morning to see all her presents. Not that there had ever been much under the tree for her. Not that they'd even had many Christmas trees. Her mother, Magnolia, rarely even acknowledged the holiday. But this time it wasn't presents she was looking forward to, it was family. Lots of family. And Walker's family had practically adopted her as one of their own.

Violet walked over to the Christmas tree by the front window. "Rob came in and told me it's too soon to put up the tree. It's a live tree. Do you think it's too soon? Will it last through Christmas? I can't wait to decorate." She motioned to a stack of boxes in the corner. "I found some decorations, but they need to be pitched. They're in pretty sorry shape."

"I don't think it's too soon. I saw they had the tree lot set up in town already. Walker is going to help me pick out one for my cottage. I haven't ever had my own Christmas tree." She'd never been able to afford one—no, there had been one. It was more like a branch, though. A cutting someone had thrown out that she found and rescued. She'd carefully made cut snowflakes out of paper to hang on it. But this year? This year she was having a real tree. Real ornaments. She'd already started making some homemade ones from ideas she'd found on Pinterest. Not that hers looked quite as nice as the ones online, but she loved making them.

"I'm going to go to Parker's and buy new lights for the tree, and I want to put them around the windows too. I'm so excited about Christmas this year."

"The wharf has had the lights and decorations up for weeks. And they are lighting the big tree at the wharf entrance tomorrow."

"I don't want to miss that either. I think I'll put a sign up on the office that evening too. And I should tell all our guests about it. I bet they won't want to miss it."

"I can't wait. And did you see the storefronts downtown? They're all decorated for the holidays. I swear, this town is magical this time of year." More excitement trilled through her. Her life was so full of happiness these days. She never thought she'd live a life like this. Family. Love. A place where she could put down roots.

"I think I'll go set up for happy hour. And

you're working at Jimmy's tomorrow morning, right?"

"Yes."

Violet headed out the door and Aspen stood by the reception desk. She couldn't believe her luck at landing the job at Jimmy's on the Wharf, the restaurant that Walker's family owned. And that's where she met Walker. When her whole life started to fall into place.

She crossed over and opened the small closet, grabbed the broom, and headed out to the front porch. She'd just sweep off the porch and enjoy the gorgeous weather Florida was providing for them. Yes, she was lucky to have this job and the one at Jimmy's. Lucky to have Violet for a friend. And very, very lucky to have found Walker.

She hummed a Christmas carol under her breath as she swept the long planks. Yes, it was going to be the perfect holiday season this year.

CHAPTER 3

Danny unpacked his suitcase, hanging up some shirts and placing clothes in the dresser. He hated living out of a suitcase so he always unpacked completely whenever he traveled. When he finished, he headed out of his room. The door across the hall to Allison's room was firmly closed. Music filtered out, but not too loud. Great, because he didn't think he had it in him to tell her to turn it down so it wouldn't disturb others.

She'd probably give him the look, anyway. The look that said he was making impossible demands of her. Like coming here to Moonbeam, a beautiful beach town. Such a sacrifice. He shook his head.

Suspended. He still couldn't believe she'd managed to get suspended from school. And had shown up drunk at school. How did she think she would get away with that? Underage drinking. Hadn't he talked to her endlessly about that? How he wouldn't put up with it. The dangers. Drinking and driving. Obviously he needed to keep a better eye on her.

He hardly recognized this sullen teenager. Where was the cute little girl who would run to him and wrap her arms around him in a hug?

Allison barely said two words a day to him now. He'd tried. He really had. Met with the school counselor four times this year already. Tried taking her to a professional therapist. Read countless books on parenting teenagers. But he was a failure.

He knew she missed her grandmother terribly. His mother had practically been like the mother Allison never would have. Her death had taken a terrible toll on both of them. He got that. But Alli was a smart girl with so much potential. She just seemed to have lost her way.

Maybe this break, far away from her friends, would be good for her. He stood in the front room of the cottage and looked around. It was a cheerful room full of coastal decor, currently illuminated by the late afternoon sun filtering in through the window. He spied a coffeemaker on the counter, along with a container of coffee. Good, because he needed his coffee in the morning.

He walked over to the window and gazed out into the courtyard. A few people were beginning to gather around a table set up across the way. Violet's happy hour was starting. It looked preferable to being here in the cottage with a daughter who wasn't speaking to him.

He headed back to Alli's room and knocked on the door. "Alli, there's a happy hour out in the courtyard. Want to come?"

Silence.

"Allison?"

"I'm not going to some stupid happy hour. And I can't drink, remember?"

"There's soda and snacks. Don't you want to come meet people? Maybe some kids your age are staying here."

"Not interested."

He let out a long sigh. He was always sighing these days. "Okay, suit yourself. I'm going to go. I'll just be right out in the courtyard."

He headed outside and crossed over to where people were gathering.

"Hi, Danny, come join us." Violet waved him over. "Let me introduce you. This is my brother, Rob, and his wife, Evelyn."

Rob reached out a hand. "Good to meet you. Violet said you're here with your daughter through the holidays."

"I am." He shook Rob's hand. "She's sixteen and I couldn't convince her to come out and join us."

"Oh, my niece is about that age. If you come by Sea Glass Cafe tomorrow, Emily is working. I'll introduce them." Evelyn smiled. "It's always nice for kids to have friends to hang out with."

Maybe. But that depended on what kind of friends they were. The past few months had sure proven that.

"Okay, we'll do that." If he could convince Alli to leave her room. And he wasn't quite certain he was willing to let her hang out—out of his sight—with kids her age. Who knew what trouble she might get herself into?

"You should go for breakfast. Best thing ever. Evelyn is the chef there, and I heard a rumor she's making her cinnamon rolls for tomorrow's breakfast." Rob grinned. "Pretty sure I'm having my breakfast there too."

Evelyn smiled at her husband. "I am making cinnamon rolls."

"Sold. We'll be there." Well, at least *he'd* be there. He had no clue if Alli would join him. He could always bring her back some breakfast. He wondered if he'd have to bring her all her meals. If she'd just sit in her room for weeks.

No, you're the parent. You can tell her she needs to come out with you. Do things.

He missed the old Alli. The friendly one who loved to hang out with her dad.

"Do you want something to drink?" Violet asked and motioned to the table. "A cabernet and a chardonnay. Beer in that cooler, soda and water in that one." She pointed to the coolers beside the table.

"I'll just grab a soda." He went over and retrieved one, popped the tab, and took a swallow. He filled a plate with appetizers from the overflowing spread of food.

Evelyn smiled at him as he returned to their group. "Oh, and I meant to tell you. There's a tree lighting tomorrow night too. Right at the entrance to the wharf. It's really fun. They have hot chocolate and cookies afterward. And they have on all the lights and decorations on the wharf. It's really something to see. You should bring your daughter."

"That sounds like fun." But Alli might think it was boring. She thought everything was boring and rolled her eyes at him every time he suggested they do something together. "I'll see if she wants to come."

"Great. We have constant activities leading up to Christmas. Music on the wharf. A bake sale with a cookie baking contest. Oh, and a gingerbread house building competition," Evelyn added.

"This is my first Christmas in Moonbeam and I can't wait to see everything." Violet laughed. "I keep reminding myself that I still have to run the resort while trying to do all the Christmassy things."

Guilt ran through him when he realized he hadn't really done much for Alli for Christmas since his mother had died. He bought her what she wanted. They had a tree. But that was about it. Maybe a town that pulls out all the stops for Christmas was just what they needed. "Sounds like the town goes all out for Christmas."

"We do." Evelyn nodded. "It's a magical time of the year here."

"This is my first Christmas here too." Rob slipped his arm around Evelyn, glancing at her with adoring eyes. "I can't wait to spend it with my beautiful wife."

Evelyn blushed. "Stop it."

"Hey, I'm only telling the truth." Rob leaned down and brushed a kiss on her cheek.

A pang of envy stabbed him, surprised him. He'd never had that with Linda. Or with any woman. Just the comfortable feeling of being together and knowing you were loved.

Violet laughed. "And there you have it. Robbie always tells the truth. Always has an opinion."

Rob laughed. "Even when my sister doesn't want to hear it."

She hip-checked him and grinned. "Because you have way too many opinions."

More envy swept through him. Danny was sorry he'd never had that. A sibling. One to tease with. He'd always wished he had a big family. And Alli would never have that either. Things might have been different if Linda had stayed. If they'd had another child. If, if.

But life was what it was now. And he was

determined to make the best of it. See if he could find some common ground with Alli again. Or at least get her to say more than one- or two-word sentences to anything he asked her.

CHAPTER 4

To Danny's surprise, Alli said yes to going to Sea Glass Cafe the next morning. Maybe she was just starving, since all she'd had for dinner last night was the plate of appetizers he'd brought her. She did gripe a bit when he said they were going to walk there. He'd looked the cafe up on his phone and it was fairly close. He wanted to get out and explore the town a bit. She reluctantly agreed to walk.

Not that she said more than a few words the whole time. If he said something or asked a question, he got single-word answers or a nod. She rolled her eyes no less than three times while they strolled along the sidewalks.

When they walked into Sea Glass Cafe,

Evelyn was standing near the door. "Oh, great, you came."

"Evelyn, this is my daughter, Allison."

"Allison, nice to meet you."

He eyed Allison who thankfully managed to get out a "Nice to meet you too."

"Why don't you grab that table by the window? I'll send Emily over to wait on you." Evelyn turned to Allison. "She's my niece. Great-niece. She's about your age."

They sat at the table, and Evelyn disappeared through a door in the back. A young girl bustled out from the back and headed to their table, a welcoming smile on her face.

"Good morning. Aunt Evelyn says you're staying at Blue Heron Cottages through the holidays. Moonbeam is a great place to spend Christmas. We really go overboard. You'll be glad you came to town." She handed them menus. "I'm Emily."

"I'm Danny, and this is Allison."

"Hi." Allison actually said another word.

"We have cinnamon rolls this morning. You shouldn't miss them. And everything is really great. Aunt Evelyn is a really good cook." Emily waved to some guests coming in. "I'll be back to take your order. Let me seat these customers."

He looked over the menu, and everything sounded delicious. "What looks good to you?" He looked over the top of the menu at Allison.

"I'll have the fruit and yogurt."

"No cinnamon roll?"

She glared at him. "So I can't pick out my own meals now?"

He held up a hand. "Of course you can." Was everything going to be an argument? He couldn't say anything right.

Emily hurried back over. "Are you ready to order?"

He ordered his breakfast with a cinnamon roll on the side. Allison ordered her yogurt.

"You sure you don't want to try the cinnamon roll? They really are the best," Emily said.

"Okay, sure, I'll have one."

Guess it just took the right person to suggest it...

"Coffee?"

"Yes." He nodded.

"I'll have some too," Allison said and looked at him defiantly to see if he'd squash her order. Since when did she drink coffee?

Emily returned with the coffee and poured them both cups. Allison dumped in three creamers and two packets of sugar. He barely kept from grimacing at that as he sipped his black coffee.

They sat in silence. He wasn't sure what he could say that wouldn't irritate her. At least with the silence, she wasn't glaring at him.

But the silence finally got to him. "So, do you want to go to the beach today?"

"Nah."

"If we stop by the market on the way home, we could pick up a few things to keep at the cottage. Sandwich makings, cereal, some milk. Maybe some fruit."

"I told you we should have driven." She rolled her eyes at him.

"I think we're capable of carrying a few bags of groceries with us. It wasn't a long walk."

He was rescued by Emily bringing out their meals. They sat in silence—again—as they ate. He noticed Allison ate every bite of her cinnamon roll.

Emily came over as they were finishing. "Do you want anything else?"

"Alli?"

She shook her head.

Emily took his credit card, and when she came back she was smiling. "So, you're Parkers, huh? Saw the name on your credit card. So are we. Well, kind of. We all descended from the first Parkers. The whole town calls us the Parker women." Her eyes twinkled as she laughed.

"We are Parkers."

"Wonder if we're some kind of distant relation."

"Our Parkers are from Minnesota."

"Ah." Emily nodded and handed him back his credit card. "So, I guess not."

He slipped the card back into his wallet.

"There's a tree lighting at the wharf tonight. A bunch of us are going. Do you want to join us? It's pretty cool." Emily looked at Allison, then at him. "If it's okay with your dad."

"Can I?" Allison stared at him as if daring him to say no... or to say yes. She was grounded, after all.

But Emily seemed like a nice girl. And she worked in her family's cafe. Seemed like a hard worker. It would probably be all right to let Allison go. And honestly, it would give both of them a break from the tension. "Sure, she could meet you there."

Allison's eyes widened. "Really?"

He nodded. For the first time in a very long time, he saw a smile on Alli's face.

41

"I'll meet you by the entrance to the wharf. Say seven o'clock."

"Sounds great." Alli nodded vigorously.

"We'll be there."

She glanced over at him and frowned. "You're not going to hang around, are you?"

He shook his head. "I'll see if I can meet up with some of the people I met last night. Violet said she's going."

Allison looked relieved.

"Okay, I'll see you then." Emily hurried over to wait on another table.

"I thought I was grounded."

"You're grounded from your friends at home. And you'll be grounded here if I find out you get into any trouble. Grounded for the rest of your life. I'm going to trust you tonight."

She nodded. "It'll be fine."

He only hoped she was telling the truth.

CHAPTER 5

Violet hung a sign in the window of the office saying she was at the tree lighting festivities and left her cell phone number if any guest had an emergency. But she was fairly certain they were all going to the tree lighting too. She headed into town and reached the wharf about seven. Townspeople were milling around, laughing, talking.

She spied Danny standing alone by the hot chocolate table and went over to him. "You made it." She smiled and reached for a cup of the free hot chocolate.

"I did. And Allison is here too. She met up with Emily."

"Oh, good. Emily's a great kid. Hardest worker ever. She has two jobs, plus she set up the entire history alcove in The Cabot Hotel when they remodeled and reopened."

"That certainly sounds better than the friends she was running with back home." He shook his head. "This last year has been rough."

"I'm sorry." Not that she knew anything about raising kids. Or much about teenagers, for that matter.

He glanced over to where Allison, Emily, and a group of high schoolers were standing. "She's gotten herself into a bit of trouble. I brought her here for a few weeks to get her away from her new group of friends back home in Tallahassee. And I'm hoping all the Christmas festivities will help us both find our footing again. I'm not sure if it's just the age, but we used to be so close. Now..." He shrugged. "Now I'm lucky if she says three words to me."

"And her mother?" Should she ask about her? Were they divorced?

"Her mother left us when Allison was about five. She's been in and out of Alli's life since then. More out than in."

"I'm sorry. That must be hard on Alli."

"It is. Not that she'd admit it. She's always looking for something from Linda that Linda doesn't want to give. Can't give." A sadness hovered in the corners of his eyes. "So, I try my best to be a double parent. Dad and Mom. I seem to be falling short these days."

"I'm sure it's hard being a single parent."

"It just is what it is. My mom used to help out a lot when Alli was young. But Mom passed away a few years ago."

"Oh, I'm so sorry." Danny really was a single parent with no help. She admired him for that. It had to be difficult.

The sadness in his eyes deepened. "Thank you. It's been tough."

"Maybe your trip here to Moonbeam will turn things around for both of you."

"I can only hope." He glanced over at the kids again. "She looks like she's having fun. I just saw her laugh. I haven't seen much except scowling from her in ages."

"Emily runs with a good group of friends. And her cousin, Blake, is over there too. There's this whole Parker women thing the town has, even though none of the women have the last name Parker anymore."

"Emily was telling us that they all were descended from the Parker who opened the general store."

"They are. Emily's grandmother, Donna, runs Parker's General Store now. If you need anything while you're in town, Parker's probably has it. Donna's daughter, Livy, runs Sea Glass Cafe. Emily is Livy's daughter."

He laughed. "I think I'm following all this."

"Yes, it takes a while to figure out that family. And you've met Donna's sister, Evelyn. Remember? Evelyn's married to my brother."

"So you've gotten pulled into quite a large family, it seems."

"Well, Rob has. I don't quite feel like I fit in. I mean, they always include me with Rob. But... it's Rob's family." She shouldn't feel this way. Maybe. Even though she adored everyone in the Parker women family, she couldn't help still feeling a bit like an outsider.

They both turned when they heard a voice coming from the direction of the tree. The mayor said a few words.

"Do you think they're going to have a countdown like they do in all those Christmas movies?" She leaned close to Danny to ask.

"I certainly hope so." The soft crinkling of his eyes accentuated the boyish grin he gave her.

In another minute, the countdown began.

She joined in, enjoying the fun. "Ten, nine, eight…"

Danny winked at her as he joined in. "Seven, six, five."

"Four, three, two, one!" The lights blinked on and the crowd cheered and clapped. The tree sprung to life with multicolored lights illuminating the ornaments covering its branches. A bright star shone from the top.

They stood admiring the tree, and she soaked up the joy swirling around in the crowd. She'd never seen anything so magical. "Oh, this is just so great. Better than I imagined. And I heard there are decorations along the walkway on the wharf too. Do you want to go see them?"

"I certainly do. Though I don't think they could top this tree lighting. I've never been to one. But I can definitely say I'm a fan now."

"Oh, me too. It was fabulous." She led the way to the entrance of the wharf and they wandered down the wide walkway. Twinkle lights were strung across from the stores lining each side of the walk. More trees were scattered around along with lighted characters. A Santa and elves. Rudolph and a snowman.

"Look—" Danny pointed. "They even have

a group of lighted dolphins jumping over wrapped presents."

"Only in Moonbeam." She laughed. "You want to go grab a drink at Jimmy's? It's at the end of the wharf. Then I probably need to head back."

"Sure, that sounds good. Let me text Allison."

They headed into Jimmy's, and Aspen greeted her with a hug, her eyes shining. "Did you see it? Walker and I went to see it. It was so magical."

"That's exactly how I'd describe it." Violet hugged Aspen back. "We're going to have a great Christmas, aren't we?"

"We are."

"Danny, this is Aspen. She works the desk at the cottages and works here at Jimmy's."

"Great to meet you." Danny nodded in greeting. "And I have to agree with both of you. It was kind of magical. I'm glad Allison got to see it."

"Allison is his daughter," she explained to Aspen. "Anyway, we're here for a quick drink."

"There are a few open seats at the bar."

"Okay, thanks." She and Danny headed to the bar and climbed onto barstools.

Walker came over. "Hey, Violet. Did you come to see the tree lighting?"

"I did. It was great."

"Aspen said that you might just post a sign on the office door that you were at the lighting. Glad you did. It's not to be missed."

"Walker, this is Danny, one of our guests."

"Good to meet you, Danny. What will you have?"

"A beer."

"We've got a good local craft wheat beer."

"Sounds perfect."

"I'll have one too."

Walker grabbed their drinks and returned with them in frosty mugs, along with a bowl of nuts and pretzel mix. "Enjoy."

She took a sip of the cold amber liquid. "Ah, this is really good."

"It is." Danny nodded.

Just then, Emily, Allison, and Blake walked up to them.

"Dad, they invited me to go to a bonfire on the beach. Can I go?"

The boy reached out a hand. "I'm Blake, Mr. Parker."

"Nice to meet you." Danny shook his hand. "But I'm not sure about the bonfire…"

"Oh, come on, Dad. You can't keep me locked up forever."

He sighed. "Tell me where it is, and I'll come get you at ten o'clock."

"Ten. That's way too early." Allison glared at him.

"No, ten is fine. I have to be home a little after that, anyway," Emily said. "Blake and I can walk her back to the cottages if that's okay."

Danny didn't look totally convinced but still nodded. "Okay, but seriously Allison. Do not be late."

"She won't, sir," Blake said. Then the three of them disappeared.

"Hope I made the right decision. She's grounded back home. Mostly because I don't want her hanging out with her new group of friends."

"She'll be fine here. Emily and Blake are responsible kids. They won't get into any trouble."

"I hope not." He frowned into his glass, looking lost in thought.

She wondered just what kind of trouble Allison had gotten into but didn't want to pry.

"I should finish up and get back to the

cottages. Make sure everything is okay there for the night."

"I'll walk you back if that's okay."

"You sure you don't want to stay here and browse around?"

"I'm sure." He took the last swallow of his drink and slipped off the stool, laying money on the bar for their drinks.

"I can get my own."

"I've got it. You did provide happy hour yesterday, after all."

"Fair enough." She slid off her stool, and they wove their way through the tables and back out to the wharf.

Danny strolled beside Violet along the walkway between the shops on the wharf. It was nice to have someone to share a drink with, take a walk with. That was an unexpected perk to this trip.

Two older women—identical twins— stopped them. "Well, Violet. Look at you out and about. Glad you could make it to the lighting," one of the women said.

"And who is your date?" the other woman asked.

"Oh, he's not my date. He's staying at the cottages. I just ran into him here at the tree lighting," Violet rushed to explain. "Jackie, Jillian, this is Danny Parker."

"Like the Parker women? Any relation to them?"

"No, no relation. But I'm pleased to meet you ladies." He had no clue who was Jackie and who was Jillian. They looked identical, dressed identically, and even were carrying the same purse.

"Nice to meet you." One of them bobbed her head. "You sure this isn't a date?"

"No, ma'am. Just a friendly drink after the tree lighting."

"If you say so." The other twin looked at him skeptically.

"Did you enjoy the tree lighting? This was my first time seeing it. It was wonderful." Violet changed the conversation.

"It always is. That's one thing we do well in Moonbeam. We have a wonderful Christmas season. So many activities."

"Jackie and I are entering the cookie baking contest."

"We're using an old family recipe."

"I hope we win. Wouldn't that be nice?" Jillian said. "Are you going to enter, Violet?"

"Me? Oh, no. I'm not much of a baker."

"Oh, such a shame. The contest is such fun. Though I imagine Evelyn will enter, so the competition will be tough."

"I expect so." Violet nodded. "Well, we should be going. Got to get back to the cottages. Nice to see you two."

"You too. And nice meeting you, Danny." Jackie gave him one long, last appraising look.

He and Violet continued toward the entrance. "That, my friend, was the Jenkins twins. Famous for spreading gossip. Don't be surprised if people around town start asking you if we're dating."

"Really? I thought you made it clear we just happened to see each other here." It was definitely not a date. He didn't date. Too busy with work and hated to be gone at night on a date, especially with Allison getting into trouble.

"The Jenkins twins think what they want to think. And tell everyone they see what they think too."

"If I see them again, I'll straighten them out."

Violet chuckled. "Good luck with that."

They headed down the sidewalk toward the cottages. It had turned a bit chilly since the sun had set. Violet shivered slightly.

"You cold?"

"A bit. I know better. I should have grabbed a sweater."

"Here, take my jacket." He shrugged it off and slipped it around her shoulders.

"Thanks. But now you'll be cold."

"I'm fine." He was, in fact, a bit chilly, but he wouldn't let on. Besides, his jacket looked good on her, if too big. And it seemed just natural to be walking with Violet. Something friends would do. He hadn't really made friends since he and Allison had moved. Too busy. But even though he'd just met Violet, she felt sort of like a friend to him. And he liked that. He'd take a sort of friend over no friends.

She held onto the edges of the jacket as they walked along, in and out of the light from the streetlamps. Such a nice little town. Quaint. Friendly people. Yes, he'd made a good choice when he'd picked out this town to spend their holiday season.

Now if only Allison would enjoy being here too. Without getting into any trouble…

CHAPTER 6

Allison walked along the beach with Emily and Blake as they made their way to the bonfire. They both seemed friendly enough. And it was nice to have kids her age to hang out with. Her dad was driving her crazy with all this grounded stuff.

Then again, she'd screwed up pretty bad—not that she'd admit it to her dad. Her new group of friends did things she wasn't entirely comfortable with, but she didn't want to jeopardize the fragile friendship she had with them. It had taken over a year to make any friends at all in their new town. But it had been stupid to show up drunk at school. She was kind of embarrassed about it.

But none of the other kids had been

grounded. After it happened—the suspension—they kept texting her, asking her where she was, and she had to explain her dad had grounded her. Then, the texts stopped, and she assumed they were all back at their parties, having fun without her. Not a one of them grounded.

At least Dad had relaxed some rules here in Moonbeam. She'd actually been surprised when he said she could go with Emily and Blake. He was so impossible these days, even if she secretly understood why he was so disappointed in her.

"There it is." Emily pointed to a fire in the distance.

They continued down the beach until they reached the gathering. About a dozen other kids stood around the fire. A cooler was propped open at the far edge.

"Come on. Let's grab a drink." Blake headed toward the cooler.

Okay, then. She'd just hide the fact she was drinking from her father when she got back to the cottage. She had gotten really good at that.

She followed Blake and Emily to the cooler and plunged her hand into the icy water. Soda. Water. Another soda. She looked at Emily. "Just soda? No beer?"

"No. We're not really into that. And if I got

arrested, it might hurt my chances for college. Besides, my mom would kill me if she found out." Emily flashed a wry smile.

Okay, so this group was definitely different from her friends at home. Someone always smuggled in alcohol to their parties in Tallahassee. She grabbed a soda and popped the tab.

"You're already thinking about college?" She eyed Emily, surprised by her comment.

"Of course. I have a list of my top three choices. At least I think they're my top three. Mom and I are going to visit them so I can get a feel for what they're really like in person." She shrugged. "That's why I'm working two jobs now. Saving up money for college. Going to try and apply for some scholarships too."

"I'm going to the community college for a few years and work on my dad's boat. He owns The Destiny, an excursion boat here. He's teaching me everything about it. I got my boating license and I'm going to work toward a commercial license in a few years. But I figure business courses will help too. Who knows, maybe my dad and I will have a fleet of boats someday."

She tried not to gape at the two of them.

They were so organized. Ambitious. They knew what they wanted to do. Their next steps in life. She barely knew what her next day was going to bring. "Wow, you guys really have things figured out."

"Have you started looking at colleges?" Emily asked.

"Nah, I'm not sure I even want to go."

"That's cool. What do you want to do instead?" Blake looked at her without a hint of judgment. A welcome change from her father always harping on her.

"I don't know. I'm just not into school these days."

"What do you like to do?" Emily asked.

And that was a good question, wasn't it? She didn't even have a real answer for her. She used to like sports and choir but had dropped out of them. None of the kids in her new group of friends played sports. She used to read. Read a lot. But now... she just went out with her friends. "I like to... I don't know... just hang out." She was almost embarrassed by her answer.

"Hey, I don't think everyone needs to figure out their life when they're just a teenager. And look how many adults end up changing what

they thought they wanted to do with their life."
Emily took a sip of her soda. "My mom had me
when she was young and worked at Parker's
General Store. She recently went back and got
her degree. I'm really proud of her. She does
the business side of both Parker's and Sea Glass
Cafe."

"I think my mom always knew she wanted
to be an illustrator though. She's really
talented." Blake's eyes shone with pride. "I
didn't inherit any of her artistic skills, but I do
love to work on the boat with Dad."

"What does your dad do?" Emily asked.

"He does computer-y stuff." That was about
as close as she could describe it. He built
websites for big corporations. Shopping
systems. Rescuing companies when their
computer systems went haywire. She didn't
really know the details. Didn't *ask* the details,
she realized.

"So he can work from anywhere?"

"We just recently moved from Atlanta to
Tallahassee for his job. He used to go into the
office every day. But you know how it is now. A
lot of people work remotely. I'm sure he'll be
working a bunch while we're here." She turned
to Emily. "What do you want to study in

college?" It fascinated her that Emily already had so many plans.

"I love history. Really love it. But I'm not sure that's a viable career path. So I might study business but take as many electives in history as I can. Someday I hope to be running Parker's and Sea Glass Cafe. Just like my mom and grandmother."

How did someone her age already have her whole life figured out? College. Studies. Her future.

Another girl walked up to them and a wide smile spread across Blake's features. He gave the girl a quick hug. "Angela, you made it."

Angela smiled back at him as if he were the only person on the beach. "I was late getting out of work, so I missed the tree lighting."

"Angela, this is Allison. She's staying at Blue Heron Cottages through the holidays," Emily introduced her.

"Hey." She smiled at Angela and wondered if she, too, had her whole life figured out.

Blake dropped an arm around Angela's shoulders. Okay, so they were a couple. She wondered if Emily had a boyfriend.

Blake looked at his watch. "We still have time to hang out before we need to walk you back to the cottages. Don't worry. We won't miss your curfew."

"Yes, if we get you back on time, maybe you can hang out with us some more while you're here."

"That would be great." Much preferable to hanging out with her dad with his judgmental eyes.

CHAPTER 7

Danny was up early the next morning, sipping on coffee and reading the news on his computer. He was starving but determined to wait for Allison to get up. Maybe she'd go to breakfast with him again.

He'd been mildly—but pleasantly—surprised when she showed up on time last night. Blake had walked her up to the door. He seemed like a nice young man. Danny had asked Allison about her evening, but all she'd said was it was fine. You know, her typical one-word answer.

His stomach growled, but he ignored it and poured another cup of coffee, wondering how late Alli would sleep in. Around ten, she finally came out of her bedroom.

"Morning." He smiled at her, hoping to get a smile in return. Or at least not get a scowl.

She nodded. Guessed that was as good as he was going to get.

"Want to go grab breakfast?"

"Yes, can we go back to Sea Glass Cafe? Emily said she was working again today."

Wow, how many words was that? "We sure can," he quickly answered before she could change her mind. "Do you want me to drive this time?"

"Nah, we can walk. Emily says they walk everywhere here in Moonbeam."

"Okay, then. You ready?"

Alli nodded.

They headed out of the cottage. Violet was sweeping the porch of the office as they walked past. "Morning, Danny. Morning, Allison," she called out.

"Morning." They walked up to the office porch. "I had a great time at the tree lighting last night. Thanks for the company."

"My pleasure." Violet's brown eyes sparkled with genuine warmth. She was wearing shorts and a bright pink t-shirt that said Moonbeam on it. Her chestnut-colored hair was pulled back and caught in a clip.

"We're headed into town for breakfast at Sea Glass Cafe again."

Violet leaned the broom against the wall and stepped to the edge of the stairs. "Hard to get enough of Evelyn's cooking, isn't it?"

"It is."

"Allison, did you have a good time with Emily and Blake last night?"

Allison nodded. "We had fun."

Oh, look. Violet could get three-word answers out of Allison. Lucky woman.

"I'm glad."

"We better go. I'm starving," Danny said.

"Hate to have one of my guests starve." Violet grinned at him. "Oh, and late afternoon I'm going to set up the croquet set out in the courtyard if you two want to come out and play."

"Haven't played croquet since I was a boy. I'd love to. Allison?"

"Maybe."

With a wave, he led the way down the walkway and they headed into town. He asked more questions about last night but only got one-word answers. But at least she seemed fairly agreeable. Not sulking or flat-out mad at him. That was an improvement.

They went into the cafe and Emily waved to them from across the room. "Take a seat anywhere," she called out.

They grabbed a table in the corner, and Emily came over with a pot of coffee and menus. "We're slammed today. And one of our servers, Jake, got called away. His grandma got hurt, and he went up to Charleston to help her out for a few weeks." She spun around, gave a one-minute sign to a neighboring table, and turned back to them to pour them both a cup of coffee. "I'll give you a minute to look over the menu. I'll be right back."

Emily hurried away. She took another table's order, poured coffee for yet another table, then scurried back to the kitchen.

"She's a hard worker." He waited for Allison's nod or one-word answer.

"You know what? She already has a list of colleges she's looking at with her mom. Knows what she wants to study. So does Blake. I've never seen kids with their lives so planned out."

He was pleasantly surprised by her conversation. Like she'd actually *started* a topic of discussion with him. He knew he'd better tread carefully. "They do?"

"Yes, and Blake is going to work for his dad.

He owns an excursion boat here in town. It goes out in the harbor and out to an outlying island."

"We could maybe see about booking a ticket for one of the trips."

"I'd like that." She smiled at him.

Allison. Smiled. At. Him.

His heart soared at this tiny glimpse of the Allison he used to know. Emily hurried over. "Ready to order?"

"I'll have a cinnamon roll," Allison ordered.

"Two eggs, fried. Hashbrowns. Bacon. And a cinnamon roll."

"I'll have some bacon too." Allison handed her menu to Emily.

Emily grinned. "You can't ever go wrong with adding bacon to an order." She turned at the sound of more customers coming in and shook her head. "Having lots of customers is great for the cafe, but I don't want them to get annoyed if I'm not getting to all of them quickly enough. But I guess it's just going to be this way for the next few weeks until Jake gets back."

"I could help out."

His mouth dropped open, and he stared at Allison.

"I mean, I don't have any experience waiting tables, but you could teach me. I can clear tables and deliver the food and do whatever else you need."

"Really? That would be great! The pay is fair and the tips are usually good. I'll let my mom know. Can you fill out some paperwork after breakfast?"

"Yes."

"Perfect. I'll go put your order in and tell Mom."

Emily hurried away. He stared at Allison. "You're taking a job?"

"Yes. I'm sixteen. I'm old enough."

"I know you are. You just never showed any interest in…" He caught himself just in time.

"In working? I know. But Emily works two jobs. Saving money for college. I mean, I don't have any plans to go to college, but it would be nice to earn some spending money. And it will give me something to do while I'm here." Allison fiddled with the salt shaker. "It's okay that I said I'd do this, isn't it?"

"Of course. But you still need to get your schoolwork finished and turned in."

"I will. But you're going to be working too, aren't you?"

"Yes. But I hope we can still find time to just… hang out. Like we used to."

"We'll see. I might be busy working."

He smothered a smile. "Yes, you might be."

And just like that, he had a smidgeon of hope that Allison was going to be okay. This split from her friends back in Tallahassee had been a good decision on his part. Maybe, just maybe, they'd find their way back to how they used to be.

"You want me to check into tickets on Blake's dad's boat?"

"Let me see when Emily needs me to work first, but then, yes. Let's go on the boat. I'd like to see what it's like."

He nodded. "Great. I'll check into it, and you can let me know after you find out your shifts."

They finished their breakfasts, paid the tab, and Allison rose from the table. "I'm going to go back in the kitchen and fill out the paperwork they wanted me to sign. Is it okay if I work today if they need me?"

He nodded. "Just text me what you're doing and when you'll be back to the cottages."

"I will." She disappeared into the kitchen, and he rose, heading out into the sunshine on Magnolia Avenue. He looked up and down the street, wondering what he'd do now with his unexpected free afternoon.

He saw a bookshop down the street and headed that direction. Maybe he'd find himself a good book to read. When was the last time he'd taken time to read a book? He headed toward the bookstore.

A woman greeted him as he entered. "Hello, welcome to Beachside Bookshop. Can I help you find something?"

"I think I'll just browse around a bit."

"That's fine. If you need help, just let me know."

He browsed the shelves for fifteen minutes or so, picking out a book for himself. Then he spied a new release from an author Allison used to read all the time—not that he ever saw her read these days—but he picked it up too. He headed to the checkout.

"Oh, good choices." The woman smiled at him.

"My daughter and I are staying at Blue Heron Cottages through the holidays. Thought we might get in some reading."

"Oh, Violet's place. She's done a great job remodeling the resort. I'm Collette, by the way.

This is my bookshop." She handed him the package.

"I'm Danny. Nice to meet you."

"Oh, Violet's friend? Did you enjoy the tree lighting last night?"

"Violet's friend? Well, I did run into her at the tree lighting and had a drink at Jimmy's."

Collette flashed a friendly grin. "So I heard when the Jenkins twins came in earlier today."

He laughed. "Violet said they'd be spreading rumors."

"They don't mean any harm. They just keep tabs on... well, on everyone and everything." Her eyes twinkled. "So just be prepared for more people to know you and Violet were together."

"Thanks for the warning." Though to be honest, he didn't care if people thought he went out with Violet. She was a charming woman. Fun. Easy to talk to. And having a friend in town was nice.

"Come back again if you need more to read."

"Thanks, Collette. I'll be back if we finish these."

This town was filled with friendly people. He liked that. Back in Tallahassee, he barely even knew his neighbors. Here, Allison had made friends with Emily. He'd made friends with Violet. And Collette couldn't have been any more friendly.

As he headed back into the sunshine, his phone dinged. He glanced at it. Allison texted that she'd be at the cafe through the dinner shift. He wondered what time that would be and if he should come back and pick her up. Another text came through saying Blake was working tonight and he and Emily would walk her back to the cottages. So that was decided.

Looked like he was on his own for the afternoon and evening. He stopped by the market and picked up some premade sandwiches and chips. Then he chastised himself and added a bunch of items that seemed like healthier choices. That would work, and he'd have something at the cottage if Allison was hungry when she got home.

After a leisurely walk back to the cottages, he settled onto a comfortable chair on the porch and opened the book. Soon he was lost in the story and he was unaware of the time slipping by until he glanced up and saw Violet in the courtyard, the sun highlighting her rosy cheeks. He set down his book.

Violet set up the croquet set in the courtyard, carefully placing the wickets into the ground. She and Robbie had played croquet with their grandparents when they were kids, and when she first saw this flat area in the courtyard, she knew it was the perfect place for croquet. She'd found an old set in good shape at an antique store. Now she set it up a few times a week for the guests to enjoy.

Danny wandered over while she was getting the set ready. "Need any help?"

"Sure. Can you set up the crossed middle two wickets?"

"I'm on it." He placed the wickets and walked back over to her.

"Want to play a game?"

He was quick to smile. "I would. But I'm warning you, I used to be a champion player."

"I'm not so bad myself." She handed him a mallet.

They were pretty evenly matched until she knocked his ball to the very edge of the courtyard. With practiced strokes, she then sent her ball through the last two wickets and hit the stake. She raised her mallet above her head in triumph. "I win."

He shook his head and picked up his ball. "You did. I guess I need more practice."

"I've been playing nearly every week since I got the set. I'm improving. Even beat Robbie the other day, and that never used to happen." She put her mallet and ball back in the wooden stand. "Would you like some lemonade? I made up a pitcher."

"Love some."

He followed her back to the office and remained outside while she went to retrieve the pitcher of lemonade and two glasses. She filled the glasses and handed him one.

"Want to sit?" She motioned to the chairs lining the porch.

He sank onto a chair and she took the one beside him. Then she popped up, leaned over the railing, and plucked a dead gardenia bloom from one of the plants lining the porch.

"Got to keep them looking nice," she said, then sat back down next to him. "They bloom in the summer mostly, but random blooms pop up now and then. I love their scent. That was one of my favorite things about fixing up the resort. Planting the flowers and bushes around the courtyard. Just like you can't have too many Christmas decorations, you can't have too many flowers."

"The courtyard looks great. And that perfect flat space for croquet. I'd forgotten how fun it is to play. Wonder why more people don't play croquet these days?"

"Because everyone seems to be in a hurry. Always rushing around. Not taking time to just enjoy the simple things in life."

"You're probably right. Like I can't remember the last time I read a book. Picked one up at the bookshop today and started it this afternoon."

"Are you enjoying it?"

"I am. Thoroughly."

"Rob's an author."

"He is?"

"Yep. He's really a great author. But don't tell him I said that." She pressed her finger to her lips in a shushing motion as a smile teased the corners of her mouth. "It will go to his head and he already thinks he's a hotshot."

Danny set down his glass. "You two seem really close."

"We are. Especially since we both ended up here in Moonbeam. He's a great older brother, if a bit bossy with his opinions. But I adore him." She took a sip of her drink. "Do you have any siblings?"

"No, it was just me. Always wished for one though. A brother to hang out with. I was always jealous of my friends who had big, noisy families."

"Yeah, I can't imagine not having Robbie around when we were growing up. I'm younger than he is and I'm sure I annoyed him by always tagging along after him, but he rarely complained." She really was lucky to have Rob as a brother. She should tell him that more often. And Rob was lucky he married into a big family too, even if it made her feel slightly like an outsider. But that was on her because all the Parker women did nothing but make her feel welcome.

"Oh, and guess what? Allison is working at Sea Glass Cafe while we're here. She's actually working now and through the dinner shift. I can't believe she offered to do that. She's never had a job before. Never wanted one."

"She's going to work on her vacation?"

"I'm hoping it keeps her busy and out of trouble. Though she'll have to get her schoolwork finished too. She's gotten behind on her assignments and she has until the end of the semester to get caught up. Otherwise she'll need to repeat a few classes. She's a smart girl. She just didn't try very hard the last few semesters."

"Maybe Emily will rub off on her. Evelyn says she's the hardest-working teenager she's ever seen. And Blake is a hard worker too."

"Allison said they both already have plans for college and what they want to do after that."

"Emily is a planner, that's for sure."

"I hope hanging out with Emily and working with her will have a positive influence on Alli. But I hope she doesn't get so busy with work and school assignments that we don't have time to spend with each other. I miss doing things with her. She hasn't wanted much to do with me recently."

A sadness hung in the corners of his eyes. "I'm sorry. I've heard raising teens can be difficult. I'm certainly no expert, but most teens finally get over it and grow into normal adults. I mean look at us. We were teenagers once and we're pretty normal now, aren't we?" she teased, hoping to make him smile.

He rewarded her with a grin. "Yes, I guess we are." He relaxed back into his chair and stretched out his legs. "Well, I'm normal," he teased back.

She laughed. "Getting a bit competitive, are we? That happens when I soundly thrash you at croquet, I guess."

"I wouldn't say you thrashed. It was very close." His eyes twinkled and his features relaxed.

He was so easy to talk to. She was enjoying spending time with him. Before she knew what she was doing, she blurted out, "Would you like to go to dinner tonight? Aspen is working the desk. I was thinking of going out to grab something. You said Allison was working tonight. We sure don't want you to go hungry."

"That sounds like a good idea. Could we go to Sea Glass Cafe so I could check and see how she's doing working there?"

"Sure. Can you give me about an hour to get some things wrapped up here?" She rose and gathered their empty glasses.

"Okay, I'll pop back over here in an hour." Danny crossed the courtyard in long strides and disappeared into his cottage.

She turned to walk into the office. Now what had possessed her to ask him to go out to eat with her tonight? Except for the fact that she loved to go out to eat and rarely did because she had no one to go out with. There was Rob, but he was busy with Evelyn now. She'd gone out a few times with Rose, but Rose was back home now. She deserved a break from work every now and then, didn't she? That was all tonight was. Just friends grabbing a bite to eat. Almost convinced, she walked into her apartment attached to the office and set the glasses in the sink. Maybe she'd change clothes into something a little nicer than a t-shirt and shorts.

CHAPTER 8

Violet and Danny walked into Sea Glass Cafe. Danny couldn't help but notice that Allison rolled her eyes when she saw them. They took a table by the window and Emily brought them menus.

"Allison is a big help. She's doing everything to keep things going smoothly. Getting drinks. Clearing tables. Bringing out food. And when it was slow earlier, I was training her on actually waiting on tables. She's just what we needed while Jake is gone."

"Glad it's working out." He'd been half-afraid that Allison wouldn't work hard enough. She hadn't been putting much effort into anything these days. He scolded himself. He really shouldn't be having such negative thoughts about his daughter.

Allison came over with water glasses for them. She looked at him, then Violet. "Hi, Violet."

At least one of them got a hello.

"I heard you got a job here," Violet said. "I was headed out to eat and asked your dad to join me. Better than eating alone."

That was all this was, he reminded himself. A better-than-eating-alone dinner.

Allison turned to him, the familiar scowl on her face. "Dad, you don't need to keep checking up on me."

"I'm not—" He stopped and laughed. "Okay, I am. But the food here is great."

"You can't keep coming here every time I have a shift." She eyed him.

"I won't. Unless you're working breakfast shifts because I plan on having breakfast here often."

"You come in as often as you like." Emily grinned at him. "And I heard Evelyn is making peach muffins tomorrow. They're amazing. You don't want to miss those."

"I'll be here."

"Dad." Allison glared at him.

"Hey, it's not my fault you got a job at the place that has the best food in town."

Emily took their orders, and the girls headed away. He let out a sigh of relief. "Looks like the job is working out."

"It does."

"I'm going to tentatively try to quit holding my breath every time she's out of my eyesight."

"Can't imagine she'll get into much trouble with Emily and Blake."

"I hope not." He leaned back in his chair and stretched out his legs. They brushed against hers. "Oh, sorry."

She moved her legs over a bit. "No problem."

"Enough talk about my parenting woes. Let's talk about you. So how long have you owned the resort?"

"Just bought it this year. Had to remodel everything. It was really run down. Rob helped with a lot of it. Then the whole town came over and helped finish things up when I took a silly fall and broke my arm. I love this town. They all jumped in when I needed them."

"I was just thinking earlier today about how

friendly the town is. I bet it's different living in a small town."

"It is. At first, I didn't quite feel like I fit in. But soon I made friends and started the Friday happy hour, and met so many people. I love running the resort."

"You did a good job with it. I never would have believed it had been run down. It's charming."

A blush crept across her cheeks at the compliment. "Thank you."

He leaned forward and grinned. "And guess what? You were right. The twins have been spreading the news that we were together last night."

She laughed. "We better hope they don't see us tonight, or we'll be a permanent couple in their minds."

Which they weren't, of course. He was just here through the holidays. So that was impossible. But it was nice to have a friend to hang out with while he was here since it appeared Allison wasn't going to have much time to spend with him.

Allison brought out their dinner.

"Thanks." He smiled encouragingly at her.

She just nodded and hurried back to the kitchen.

Soon she came back out with a plastic tub and started clearing a nearby table. He kept an eye on her while trying not to let her see that he was. Though she glanced over at him once and rolled her eyes, so apparently he wasn't as stealthy as he hoped.

Just as she picked up the bin full of dishes, a man from the next table got up. They collided, and the bin of dishes went crashing to the floor.

"Oh, no." Allison's eyes went wide and her face turned bright red.

The cafe went silent as all eyes turned toward her.

He started to get up, but Violet placed her hand over his. "It's okay. Let her deal with it," she whispered.

And Violet was right. He should let Alli handle this, but it was all he could do to keep from rushing over there and picking up the mess.

"Sorry, miss. My fault." The man shook his head. "Should have been watching where I was going."

Allison still stood there, frozen in place. Emily hurried up to her. "Don't worry. It happens." She knelt down, picked up some broken pieces, and put them back in the tub.

"I'm so sorry. I'll pay for the dishes." Allison looked close to tears, and it wrenched his heart.

"Nonsense. It happens," Emily assured her.

"And it was my fault. I wasn't looking when I got up. Sorry about that." The man dipped his head, dropped a twenty on the table, and left.

Emily headed back to the kitchen, and Allison trailed behind, looking embarrassed.

"She looked really upset, didn't she?" He frowned.

"I think every server has dropped dishes at some point in time." Her lips curved up in a gentle smile. "And look, she got it over with on her first day."

Violet's hand still rested on his. She must have noticed at the same time because she snatched her hand away.

"Besides, that man said it was his fault. And Emily wasn't mad or anything."

He let out a long sigh. "I'm just being overprotective, aren't I?"

"A bit."

"It's just hard. She's making poor choices, then all of a sudden she pivots and takes a job. I feel like I'm being spun in a circle and I'm not sure where I'll end up."

"I guess parenting isn't easy."

"It's not. But I wouldn't trade it for anything. Allison is my whole world."

CHAPTER 9

The next morning, Violet cleaned up the reception area then went out to sweep the porch, missing Rose and their daily morning coffee. Rose should be back in a few days, though, and she couldn't wait to see her.

She swept the porch with slow, measured strokes. It was soothing somehow, this familiar morning chore. She glanced over toward Danny's cottage. She'd had a good time at dinner last night. He was fun to be with. They'd split the bill, so it hadn't been a date. And at least they hadn't run into the Jenkins twins again, so no more rumors would be floating around.

She continued with her slow sweeping.

Danny sure was worried about Allison. But that was probably just how parents felt most of the time. She wondered what it would be like to feel like that. To have a child. Watch the child grow up. Worry about them. She'd never have that. She was too old for it now. Just something that wasn't meant to be a part of her life. Most of the time, it didn't really bother her. At least not much. Of course she didn't dwell on it much either. She had a good life just like it was. Especially since buying the resort and Rob moving here too.

A man she didn't recognize crossed the courtyard heading toward the office and it broke her train of thought. He wasn't one of their guests. An older gentleman with gray hair and an ambling gait. There was a friendly smile on his features and a twinkle in his blue-gray eyes as he walked up to her. "Morning," he said.

"Good morning. May I help you?"

"Just wanted to drop by and say hi. I bought the house next to your resort. Right next to the peach-colored cottage. I'm George Westchester."

"Nice to meet you, Mr. Westchester."

"Nah, it's just George. Been just George since I retired some years back."

"Well, George, I'm Violet."

"My realtor said you recently bought this place. I came here a couple of times years ago when it was Murphy's Resort." He laughed. "It's a lot nicer now. Way nicer. I really like the brightly painted cottages."

"Thank you. I've worked hard to get it remodeled and up and running."

"You did an impressive job."

"So, did you just move in?"

"I did. A couple of days ago. Just getting settled in." He gave her a wry smile. "Well, that's not quite right. My things are here, but I'm a bit overwhelmed with the unpacking."

"Unpacking and figuring out where everything goes is a big job."

"I guess there's really no hurry. I've got nothing but time on my hands these days."

"Well, if you need anything, just pop in here and ask. Be glad to help. The whole town helped me get the resort ready to open. I'm always willing to return the favor."

"I'll be sure to ask if I need anything."

"Oh, and on Fridays I have a happy hour here for our guests. Quite a few people from town drop by too. You should come. I'll introduce you to more people."

"I'll do that. I'd like to get to know more people here in Moonbeam. I haven't really met anyone yet."

"I'll see you on Friday then."

He bobbed his head. "Friday. And thanks for the invite." He turned and crossed the courtyard, then disappeared down the beach.

Nice man. She'd love to help him get to know more people. Help him start to feel like he fit in. Like she was just starting to feel herself. Sort of.

She headed back in to get caught up on ordering supplies. Her concentration broke when she heard the door open. She spun around and clapped her hands in delight. "Rose. You're back."

A big grin spread across Rose's face, and she opened her arms. Violet hurried over, and Rose enveloped her in a much-welcomed hug. "I've missed you, Violet. I know I wasn't gone long, but it seems like it was forever."

"I was just thinking this morning how much I missed having my morning coffee with you. And talking to you. And just... well, everything. It's so great to have you back."

"I know I'm a few days early, but I called

yesterday and Aspen said the peach cottage was available. I told her not to tell you so I could surprise you."

"And you did. I'm so glad you're back."

"And look, you have the tree up. It looks wonderful."

"It's begging me to get lights on it and decorate it. I just haven't found the time."

"Then it's good I'm back. I'll help you."

"I'd love that. It's more fun to decorate with other people instead of alone."

A sadness flitted across Rose's features. "It is. I didn't put up a tree back home. I just couldn't face doing it alone."

She reached over and took Rose's hand. "I'm sure it's hard. Different."

"It is. But I'm dealing with it. It helps that I can be here with you and all the people I've met here in town for Christmas."

"I can't imagine having Christmas without you."

"It feels great to be back. I can't wait to get settled in." Rose smiled. "But first, I don't suppose you have time for that cup of coffee now, do you?"

Violet laughed. "I sure do." She poured

them each a mug, and they headed outside to the porch and settled onto the chairs. Now this felt right. Having coffee with Rose. Enjoying her company. It was going to be a great Christmas.

CHAPTER 10

Allison worked the breakfast shift and, annoyingly, her dad came in for breakfast. Then again, after she tried one of Evelyn's peach muffins, she couldn't really blame him. Thankfully, he left and promised not to come back for lunch. Although he didn't look very pleased about it when he heard Evelyn was making beef stew.

She and Emily cleared tables after the breakfast rush died down. She was extra careful carrying the tub of dishes back to the kitchen. Emily's mom, Livy, had assured her not to worry about the broken dishes, but she still felt bad about it.

Emily rinsed the dishes while Allison loaded

the dishwasher. Emily dried her hands. "Okay, let's sit and take a quick break."

Alli was ready for a break. She wasn't used to being on her feet so much of the day. They sat at a small table in the corner of the kitchen, both enjoying another peach muffin.

"These are so good. I'm not sure whether I like these or Evelyn's cinnamon rolls better."

"She's magic with everything she bakes," Emily agreed. "She's been showing me how to make some of it while she teaches Melody. Melody works here too, but she's off on a trip with her boyfriend, Ethan. That's why Jake's leaving hit us so hard. But you're catching on quickly."

"I hope so." Allison wanted to make sure Emily didn't think she'd made a mistake offering her the job. Besides, it was kind of fun. Chatting with customers. Keeping busy. She did have to go home after the lunch shift and work on some school assignments though. Her dad would never quit nagging her until they were all turned in. She'd stayed up late last night working on them too. She wasn't sure why she'd allowed herself to get so behind on the work. It didn't help that most of her new friends weren't that interested in doing well in school. But why had she let that influence her so much? She'd always been an A student until the move to Tallahassee.

"How come you're off school and able to work on a Monday?" She took another bite of the delicious muffin, the flavor of the peach and cinnamon delighting her tastebuds.

"It's a teacher work day, so we're off school." Emily set her muffin down. "So, do you have a boyfriend back home?"

She glanced up at Emily's abrupt change of subject. "Me? No. I mean, I dated this one guy…" She paused, wondering if she should go on. The whole thing still stung.

"And?"

She took a deep breath, a slight blush warming her cheeks. "He dumped me when I wouldn't sleep with him."

Emily frowned and shook her head. "What a jerk."

Relief swept through her at Emily's reaction. Her friends back home had called her a goody two shoes when he told everyone why he broke up with her. She'd tried to just laugh it off and said he wasn't her type. But she'd been so afraid her new friends would dump her too. Luckily they hadn't.

Was that really luck, though? She actually

was getting a bit tired of them. Partying all the time. Making rude remarks to the teachers. And then sucking her into the drinking. At first she'd hated the taste of beer, but then she got used to it. The day she got suspended, she hadn't even wanted to drink. One of the kids had swiped some hard liquor from his parents, and then they dared her to chug a large drink. Why had she let them intimidate her like that? Why was she trying so hard to fit in with a group of kids she didn't even really like?

"You okay?" Emily interrupted her thoughts.

"Oh, sorry. Just thinking about home."

"You miss your friends?"

She laughed. "That's exactly what I was thinking about. And... I don't really miss them much."

"Really?"

She shrugged. "It's kind of a nice break from them." She didn't want to explain to Emily what kind of kids she hung out with. The trouble she'd gotten into. How far behind she was in her schoolwork. Emily wouldn't understand. Or she'd think she was a loser.

She changed the subject. "Anyway, how about you? Do you have a boyfriend?"

"Nope. I'm so busy with school and my jobs, I don't know how I'd ever fit it in. Got to keep my grades up so I can hopefully get a scholarship. And work to save money. I work at The History Museum too. I really love working there. There's so much on the history of the town and the area. History fascinates me."

Emily worked two jobs and studied hard and was so determined and motivated. Doubts and embarrassment at how she'd just drifted through life the last few years swept over her. And she'd given her dad such a hard time too. A twinge of guilt that she'd been trying so hard to ignore crept through her. Right now, she wasn't really liking the person she'd become.

"I'm working at the museum later this week. You should come by and see it."

"I'd like that."

"Good. I have a shift on Thursday. Melody will be back by then, so we won't be as short-staffed."

"Will you still need me after that? After Melody comes back?" Suddenly, she didn't want to lose this job. Lose this time spent with Emily.

"Oh, we'll still need you. Especially with Christmas coming up. Seems like people get busy and eat out a lot instead of cooking at home."

Relief swept through her. "Good. You can give me all the shifts you need to. I'm enjoying working here."

"And at lunch today, I'm going to give you your own small section of tables to serve."

"You think I'm ready for that?"

"Sure do. And if you have any questions, you can just ask me. You'll do fine."

She hoped she did. She wanted to make Emily proud. Wanted to make *herself* proud of doing a good job. It sure would be a nice feeling for a change.

CHAPTER 11

On Thursday Allison headed over to the museum after her lunch shift at the cafe. Blake had been working and helped her out a few times, but she felt like she was catching on to the whole server thing pretty well. She'd met Melody this morning, who'd been more than friendly and welcoming. Livy had insisted she start calling her by her first name.

She was beginning to feel like she belonged, and it was a welcome feeling. And she didn't have to change to try to fit in like she did with her friends back home. But were they really even her friends? Not one of them had texted her since she left to see how she was doing. She'd seen some posts on social media and knew they were out partying most nights. And she realized she didn't even miss it.

She got to the museum and stepped inside. It smelled like history, if that were even possible. Like old books and memories. She shook her head at her crazy thoughts. Emily was sitting at a large table and waved to her. "Hey, come on over."

She crossed over and sank into a chair beside her. "What are you doing?"

"I'm researching the Parkers. Their history. I'm writing a paper for school on the town's history and our family's general store. Thought I'd research a few more details." Emily scribbled a note in the notebook beside her. "I found this old scrapbook someone donated to the museum. Look at all these old black and white photos. That one is of my—let me think —great, great, great grandmother. Grace Parker. The day she and her husband opened Parker's."

"That's kind of cool. We don't have many photos of our family. Dad said a fire in his grandfather's home destroyed most of the old photos and stuff. But he never met his grandfather. He died before Dad was born."

"That's too bad you don't have a lot of

family stuff. We have boxes of photos, keepsakes, and well, a ton of stuff."

"We don't. And it's just Dad and me now. My grandfather died when I was a baby. And my grandmother… she just died a bit ago."

"Oh, I'm so sorry." Emily looked up, sympathy filling her eyes. "That must be hard."

"It was." She struggled to hold back the tears she never let fall. "It is," she whispered.

"Well, I'm glad you and your dad came to Moonbeam for Christmas. Best place ever to spend the holidays. Did you know we have a Christmas boat parade each year? I'm going over to my grandmother's to watch it tomorrow night. You should come."

"I don't want to crash a family thing."

Emily grinned. "There is no such thing in our family. It's always a big group of family and friends. That's just how the Parkers are. Not that any of us have the Parker last name anymore. Don't you think it's crazy that women give up their last name when they get married? I mean, why? How did that start?"

"I guess I really never thought about it."

"I don't know if I'll ever get married, but if I do, I don't know that I'd take his last name." Emily frowned. "I think I'm going to research when all this started. My Aunt Heather took the last name Parker for her legal name. Did whatever paperwork to get it changed. She's an artist."

Allison gasped. "She's Heather Parker, the illustrator? I love her work. I have a print of hers in my bedroom at home. It's a cafe somewhere. A mother and her daughter eating ice cream cones..." She paused, not knowing why she was telling Emily all these things. "And I always thought it would be so nice to be that little girl and have her mother spend time with her like that."

Emily frowned. "Are your folks divorced? You never say anything about your mom."

"They're divorced. I don't see Mom very much. She's... busy." Which wasn't the truth. Her mother wasn't busy. She didn't work. She just didn't make time for her.

"I'm sorry. I've got family practically smothering me all the time. Though I rarely see my father. He and Mom never married." Emily shrugged. "I hardly know him. He did take me to Paris this summer, but it felt like I was in the way. He kept leaving me alone at the hotel. I ended up coming home early, and he was relieved."

"Paris. Wow."

"Yeah, it was really fun to explore and see all the history there. But Dad didn't like me going places alone, and he wasn't very interested in the museums and old churches and things like that."

So Emily had an absentee parent too. At least they had that in common. "So, do you like having such a big family? I can't imagine what it would be like."

"I do like it." Emily laughed. "Most of the time. Sometimes it seems like they know every little detail about my life. But Mom is great. She married Austin and he's cool."

She wondered what it would be like to have a big family like that. Family gatherings. Holidays together. It had always just been Gran, Dad, and her for the holidays. And now there wasn't even Gran. And last Christmas, they hadn't really done anything for the holiday. But this year was sure different.

"So you'll come to watch the boat parade? My grandmother lives right on the canal on a point. All the boats will go past it. They decorate their boats all up with lights and decorations and it's really fun. We're grilling out. We have hot chocolate and cookies and play Christmas music. Come."

"Okay. I've never even heard of a boat parade."

A wide grin spread over Emily's face. "Well, Moonbeam knows how to do Christmas. What can I say?"

CHAPTER 12

On Friday morning, Rose joined Violet for coffee on the office porch. Violet happily slipped back into their coffee routine, enjoying Rose's company.

"I finally made it to Parker's and got lights for the tree and around the windows. Do you want to help me decorate after we have our coffee?"

Rose's eyes lit up. "I sure do."

"I bought some ornaments too. Just a few. I don't want to just put up any old ornaments. I think I'll collect ones I like and then, after a few years, the tree will fill up with them."

"That's a great idea. I know people have pretty color-coordinated trees these days, but I always liked our tree with its mishmash of ornaments.

Some store-bought, some homemade. Emmett gave me an ornament each year for Christmas and made quite a few of them by hand. I loved that tradition." Rose's eyes held that sadness deep in the corners again, but she smiled. "A good memory."

"That's a wonderful tradition." She wondered how Rose would do with her first Christmas without Emmett.

"It was. I admit I brought a small box of my favorites along with me. Not that I'll have a tree in the cottage, but I just... wanted them with me."

"Oh, Rose. I'm sorry. It must be so hard. Your first Christmas without Emmett."

"These firsts are hard. But I've made it through them so far. It helps to be surrounded by friends like you though." She smiled again, the sadness lifting from her expression.

Violet was even more determined to make sure Rose had a good Christmas this year. Make sure she didn't spend too much time alone. She jumped up. "How about it? Want to get started on the tree? Let's turn on some Christmas music."

"Yes, let's." Rose stood and followed her inside.

Soon they were laughing and winding the lights around the tree. They hung the ornaments as they sang along to the familiar Christmas tunes. Finally, she got a stepladder out and placed the angel on top of the tree. They stood back and admired their handiwork.

"The tree looks lovely," Rose said.

"I think so too." She turned and grabbed a box of lights. "Now I'm going to line the windows with lights."

"Let me help."

Soon they'd strung the lights around the windows, and she hung a wreath she'd gotten at Parker's in the big front window.

"It's perfect." She grinned in delight.

Rose laughed. "I'm not sure you could even get any more lights up in here."

"I might have gone a bit overboard, but I love Christmas decorations." She tilted her head to one side. "Do you think I need a wreath in the other window in front?"

"Wouldn't hurt. You can never have too many Christmas decorations."

"Then it's decided. I'll pick up another one." And maybe just a few more decorations to put up in the office. But just a *few* more.

"I think I'll head back to my cottage." Rose set down the empty box of lights.

"You're welcome to stay here and hang out."

"I know you have work to do. And I have a good book I'm in the middle of."

"Okay, but you'll be out for happy hour, won't you?"

"Wouldn't miss it. Can't wait to see everyone."

"Evelyn and Rob are dropping by. Not sure about Melody. She just got back from her trip with Ethan. She's probably busy at the cafe. Collette said she'd stop by."

"It will be lovely to see everyone. Do you need help setting things up?"

"I wouldn't mind the help." She didn't really need it, but it was part of her mission to keep Rose busy during the holidays.

"I'll be over early then, and we'll get things ready together."

"Thanks, Rose."

Rose left the office and Violet stood back looking at all the decorations, pleased with their work. Rose was right. A person could never have too many Christmas decorations.

CHAPTER 13

Aspen counted her tips at the end of her lunch shift at Jimmy's. Better than usual today, which was great. She wanted to get Walker a really nice Christmas gift. If only she could think of what that would be...

Her phone rang, and her sister's name showed on the screen when she took it from her pocket. "Hey, Willow."

"Hi. Is this a good time?"

"Yes, just got off my shift. About to head back to the cottages."

"I have some news. And I don't know how to tell you." Her sister's voice held an edge of foreboding.

She frowned. "Just say it. What's wrong?"

"I'm afraid we can't come for Christmas after all."

Her heart sank. "You can't?" She squeezed her eyes shut.

"Derek's mother isn't doing well."

"You said she'd been ill."

"Well, she's taken a turn for the worse. All his family is coming in for Christmas now. They don't know if it will be her last one."

"Oh, I'm so sorry." Disappointment swallowed her, but then, she felt bad for feeling it. Look what Derek and his family were dealing with.

"But we'll come right after Christmas. I promise."

"Sure, I understand." She understood, but suddenly her perfect Christmas wasn't so perfect anymore. The first one that would have felt like an actual family Christmas.

"Are you okay? I'm really sorry. I was looking forward to spending it with you."

"I'm fine. Tell Derek I'll keep his mother in my thoughts. I hope she gets better."

"Thanks, Aspen. I'll talk to you soon."

The connection died, and she fought back tears as disappointment swelled over her. She needed to see Walker. Tell him about Willow. He'd make her feel better. He always did.

She found Walker and his sister, Tara, huddled over his desk in the office. Walker was on the phone and Tara was listening to his conversation. They both looked up, startled, when she knocked on the open doorway.

"I'll have to get back to you," Walker said quickly and hung up the phone.

"Oh, hey, Aspen. We were just checking... on an order mess-up." Tara gave Walker a look that Aspen couldn't quite read.

"I just wanted to say that I'm leaving now. Got a shift at the cottages." What she wanted was five minutes alone with Walker.

"Okay." Walker smiled at her, but not his usual smile. The one that said she was the only one he saw. This time there was a slight wrinkle of tension between his brows.

"So you're coming to Violet's happy hour tonight like we talked about?" Maybe she'd have to wait and talk to him this evening if he was busy with Tara now.

"Ah, no. I have to work."

She swore his name wasn't on the schedule. But then, he often came in when he wasn't technically scheduled. She tried to hide her disappointment. "Ah, okay. I guess I'll see you tomorrow then."

"Oh, we've moved the schedule around some. You're off tomorrow," Tara said as she glanced at Walker again.

"I thought I had the lunch shift."

"Nah, we're covered," Walker said as he concentrated on shuffling some papers on his desk.

"Do you have a minute to talk?" If she wasn't going to see him for a while, maybe she could have a few minutes with him before she left for the cottages.

"Actually, I'm swamped. Can we talk later?"

"Sure. I'll see you soon?" He was so busy he couldn't give her a few minutes of his time?

"Yes, of course." Walker nodded, but he didn't get up to come kiss her goodbye like he usually did.

She tamped down the trepidation that crept through her. Was he losing interest in her? Who was he talking to that he hung up on so quickly? And why did both of them look so guilty?

Tara looked at her as if waiting for her to leave.

Aspen nodded, turned, and walked through

Jimmy's. She hurried down the wharf, fighting off her fears and disappointment.

She couldn't help but think that maybe all this was coming to an end. Because people left her. That's what they did. Her mother. Her last boyfriend. Even Willow had deserted her for the holidays. And now Walker was acting strange.

The perfect Christmas she thought she'd have was crumbling right before her eyes.

"Do you think she's suspicious?" Tara asked after Aspen left.

"I don't think so." Walker frowned. "But it was awkward, wasn't it?"

"Very. You almost got caught."

"I know. It's hard to keep a secret from her." Really hard. He hadn't realized how hard it would be. And he felt guilty for hiding things from Aspen.

"Think she bought the whole moving the schedule around thing?" Tara tilted her head, eyeing him.

"I'm not sure. I guess so."

"I feel like when we were kids. Hiding

something from Mom and Dad. Like that time we broke her favorite vase."

"I do too. At least a bit." The guilt felt almost the same. He'd never been good at secrets. At hiding anything.

"And back then, Mom knew something was up. She could always tell by looking at your face. You're a terrible liar."

"I'm not sure if that's a compliment or a criticism."

"A bit of both." She laughed. "So, are you headed to town this evening?"

"I am. It's hard to find time to sneak away since I spend so much time with Aspen." He stood. "And I know I talked about me coming to happy hour at the cottages tonight. But with her tied up there, it's a good time for me to get this figured out."

"Well, I hope you get it sorted out soon. Because it's hard to cover for you."

He let out a long sigh. "I know it is. But she'll find out soon enough."

Tara nodded. "I'll keep covering for you. But I'll be glad when she knows and all this is over." She turned and left the office.

He glanced at his watch. He'd give Aspen a bit more time to make sure she'd left the wharf and got to the cottages. Just to make sure she didn't catch him in a lie. He couldn't wait to head into town.

But he'd seen the look in Aspen's eyes when she'd left. She'd been questioning him and the way he was acting. He couldn't bear to think of hurting her, but he didn't want her to find out now. The timing was off. He just had to make it through Christmas.

CHAPTER 14

Aspen seemed quiet when she came into work at the cottages. Violet wasn't sure if Aspen was tired or something was wrong. Before she could ask, a guest came in.

"I've got this," Aspen said.

"Okay, I'm going to run to Parker's. I want another wreath."

Aspen just nodded and turned to the guest.

Violet wanted everything to look perfect for when people came to happy hour tonight. She ran to Parker's and picked up the wreath, then some evergreen boughs to put on the table for happy hour. And some more lights. Then she added in some bright silver balls in a glass lantern. That would look cute on the table too.

She'd better stop or there wouldn't be room for any of the food or drinks.

She brought it all back to the cottages and carted her haul inside, dropping the packages by the door. She crossed over to the desk and looked closely at Aspen. "Are you okay?"

Aspen nodded, but Violet wasn't convinced. She swore it looked like Aspen had been crying. "Are you sure?"

A lone tear escaped and trailed down Aspen's cheek. "I'm just… disappointed. Willow called and she and Derek and Eli can't make it for Christmas. Derek's mother isn't doing well and his whole family is getting together for Christmas. It might be their last one all together."

"Oh, I'm so sorry. I know how you were looking forward to spending Christmas with them."

"I was. It was the first time I thought I'd have my family with me." She swiped at a tear. "But I shouldn't be so sad. And Derek's family needs him there. I shouldn't be so selfish. She did say they'd still come the week after Christmas.."

"I'm sorry about his mom, but that's nice that they'll still come right after the holidays."

"It is, but it won't be the same."

She hugged Aspen. "It won't. But you'll still have Walker and his family." She grinned. "And me. You can't get rid of me."

Aspen smiled through her tears. "You're right. I have lots of people to spend Christmas with. I'm just being silly."

"It's not silly to want your family to be with you during the holidays."

"Walker's family has practically adopted me, so I will have all of them." Aspen paused and frowned. "Though Walker has been acting a bit strange. I don't know. Secretive or something."

"Maybe he's just figuring out a great Christmas gift for you."

"Maybe. But I asked him to come to happy hour tonight. He wasn't on the schedule for Jimmy's. But he said he couldn't."

"Maybe something came up at work."

"You're probably right. I just wanted Christmas to be perfect."

"It still will be. And Willow will be here right afterward."

Aspen pasted on an almost convincing smile. "Yes, you're right."

"I thought I'd head out and start setting up for happy hour. You going to be okay?"

"Yes, I'm fine. Really." Her weak smile didn't inspire much confidence in her assurance.

"Okay, I'm going to hang this wreath and then head outside."

She hung the wreath, then wrestled the table outside to where she held the happy hours. Rose came over not long after she got the table set up. "You should look into getting a permanent table out here so you don't have to wrangle this one every week."

Violet stood up, stretching her back. "That's a fantastic idea. Maybe a nice weatherproof wooden one. I could paint it some bright color."

Rose laughed. "Of course you would."

"What can I say? I love bright colors."

"All the painted cottages sure make the resort cheerful."

She glanced over at Danny's cottage. "I was thinking maybe I'd get a Christmas tree for Danny's cottage. He should have one, since his daughter is with him and everything."

"Danny. The man in the pink cottage, right? You've mentioned him. Several times." Rose's eyes sparkled.

"Have I?" She looked innocently at Rose.

"And I think getting them a Christmas tree is a great idea. But we've used all the lights."

She smiled guiltily. "Not quite. I bought some more."

Rose laughed. "Of course you did."

"I wanted to put some out on the office porch railing, but I'm sure I'll still have some leftover for their tree."

"It would be a nice, friendly thing to do for them." Rose quickly hid a smile, but not before Violet saw it.

"Yes, just being nice to my guests. That's all it is." Violet turned and headed back to retrieve the cooler. She hadn't mentioned Danny *that* often, had she?

Danny couldn't get over the change in Allison since they'd come to Moonbeam. She was almost—dare he say it—friendly to him. She'd worked quite a few shifts this week and came back to the cottage and did homework after each one. Her school counselor had emailed and said Alli had turned in almost all the missing assignments. They would be graded lower for turning them in late, but at least she wasn't getting Fs on them.

She'd even agreed to go on The Destiny

with him. He'd booked tickets for early next week. The worry he'd had every time she left his sight was beginning to ebb. He'd even let her go to the movies with Emily and Blake last night. He was precariously holding on to hope that things were turning around for Allison.

The door burst open to the cottage and Allison rushed in. "Dad, you know how I went to the history museum where Emily works yesterday? It's really cool. Anyway, I was thinking. She had all these old photos of her family. We don't have any old scrapbooks or anything, do we?"

"Just a few. That fire at my grandparents took almost everything. But I could look and see what I can find in those boxes of Mom's."

Allison sat down on the chair across from him, eyeing him. "You haven't even gone through them, have you?"

Her question caught him off guard. "No... I mean, I packed them all up when I sold her house, and only kept those few boxes. But I haven't had the heart to go through them."

"How about when we go back home, we go through them together?"

Who was this girl and what had she done with his daughter?

Allison laughed. "Yes, I'm offering to help. Don't look so surprised."

"I'm not—" He shook his head. "Okay, I am surprised. And yes, I'd love to go through them with you. See if you want to keep anything."

"I just… miss her so much. It feels like there's a big hole in my heart." She blinked, and tears clouded the corners of her eyes.

"I know, honey. I feel the same way."

Allison took a deep breath, but he could tell she was still fighting back tears. And if she started crying, he wasn't sure he could keep his own tears in. "Anyway, let's look for scrapbooks and photos. Something with… history. Emily is really into her family history."

"I'm sorry I don't know more about ours. I was never really into genealogy. And Dad was an only child, so I don't really have any family on that side. Mom's sister died when she was young."

"Well, I want to learn more. Emily is researching her family and information about Parker's General Store. She's doing a paper on it for school. I'm just curious about ours." Allison stood and grabbed an apple from the bowl on the table. "I'm going to do some more schoolwork. I'm almost caught up."

She headed toward her room. He was kind of proud of himself for thinking of picking up fruit to keep at the cottage for snacks. Okay, and he'd also bought Allison her favorite flavor of ice cream. Not as a bribe, of course. Just because she liked it. He was trying so hard to make sure she had a good time while they were here. Trying to give her an actual Christmas since they'd both basically ignored the season last year. It had been easier than thinking about how much they missed his mom. But this year would be different.

He worked for another hour, then glanced at his watch. Almost happy hour time. He didn't want to miss it. He'd have a chance to see Violet again.

Now, where had that thought come from? But he realized he'd been looking forward to seeing her all day.

He walked to Allison's room and knocked on the door. "Alli, want to come to the happy hour in the courtyard?"

She came and opened the door. "I think I'm going to stay here. I really want to get all this finished so I can enjoy Christmas without it hanging over my head."

"Okay, I'll just be right outside."

"I heard Evelyn say she made some cookies for Violet for the happy hour tonight. I don't suppose you could snag me a few?"

"I sure could."

He turned and headed out of the cottage, anxious to get to the gathering. Just because he wanted to be out and among people after working in the cottage all day. That was all it was.

CHAPTER 15

Danny came out on his porch, and Violet's heart did a little skip.

No, it didn't. That was silly. And she had a firm rule not to get involved with any of her guests. Okay, she'd just made that rule. She'd never been interested in a guest before. Besides, guests came and then went away. Really foolish to get involved with someone who was leaving. Not that she was *involved* with him.

Why did her thoughts hopscotch all over the place?

She waved to him, and he trotted across the distance. "Happy Friday," he said as he walked up to her.

"Happy Friday. Is Allison coming out?"

"She's doing schoolwork. But she requested some of Evelyn's cookies."

Violet laughed. "I get appetizers and usually something sweet each Friday. Look at those cute Christmas cookies Evelyn made."

He glanced over at them. "She decorates them all up, too?"

"I think she has magical baking talents."

"I'd eat every meal at the cafe if Allison would let me."

His infectious grin made her heart skitter again. *No, it didn't.*

Unaware of her traitorous heart, he continued, "She thinks I'm checking up on her when I haunt the cafe, but I'm really just going for the food now."

Violet wasn't sure she believed him. He did seem to keep a close eye on his daughter. But that's what good parents did, right?

"I think I'll grab a beer. Want anything?" he asked.

"Sure, grab me one too."

He went to the cooler, fished out the beers, and returned, handing her one. Their fingers brushed. Not that she noticed.

Rose walked up to them, a glass of wine in her hand. "Cheers." She lifted her glass.

"Cheers," she and Danny said in perfect union.

130

"Rose, this is Danny. He's staying in the pink cottage with his daughter, Allison."

"Nice to meet you, Danny. You enjoying your stay?"

"Very much."

"Violet?"

Violet turned at the sound of her name. "George, you came. Great."

"Rose, Danny, this is George. He just bought the house right past the peach cottage. The one Rose is staying in."

George shook Danny and Rose's hands. "Nice to meet you."

"Rose is an almost permanent guest." Violet laughed. "We love having her here for the holidays. And Danny is here with his daughter."

Robbie and Evelyn walked up. "Sis, I stopped by and peeked into the office. I think you have every decoration from Moonbeam stuffed in there. And I'm not sure it's possible to have any more lights up than you have."

She wanted to stick out her tongue at him like she used to when she was a little girl, but she controlled herself. Just barely. "Ah, so you love it, right?"

He laughed. "I'd have expected no less from you. You always did love Christmas."

She turned to George. "This is my brother, Rob, the man with all the opinions. And this is his wife, Evelyn. She owns part of Sea Glass Cafe. She's the best chef. You should go there and try her cooking."

"And make sure you get there for breakfast. I swear her cinnamon rolls have some kind of magic that keeps pulling me back for more," Danny chimed in.

"I'll do that." George nodded, his eyes twinkling and a friendly expression on his face.

"Oh, and Violet. You're coming to watch the boat parade with us at Donna's tomorrow night, aren't you? You all should come." Evelyn turned to Danny, Rose, and George. "It's so magical. You should see it."

"I'm coming. I can't wait." Violet turned to Danny. "You want to come with me? And George and Rose? We could all go over together."

"I'd love to. I've heard about the boat parade, but can't quite picture it," Rose said.

"I'm in if you're sure I'm not intruding," George said.

"The more the merrier at a Parker family get-together," Evelyn assured him. "Be ready for hot chocolate and lots of Christmas cookies.

Oh, and we're grilling out hotdogs and brats. Come hungry."

Looks like she'd be headed to watch the boat parade with a whole group. And she was delighted to spend more time with Danny.

Just because he was fun and friendly. Or some other lie she was telling herself. She looked over at him and he smiled at her, an infectious look full of warmth. She quickly looked away. What was she getting herself into?

More guests came out and a handful of townspeople—who she also introduced to George—then she walked away and mingled throughout the gathering. She glanced over at where Danny was talking to Rose and George. He looked like he was enjoying himself. She'd like to spend more time talking to him, but she wanted to make sure everyone felt welcome as she circled through the crowd.

As most of the people left, she finally made it back to Danny. No, she made it back to *Rose*. Danny just happened to be in the same spot.

"Nice crowd tonight. It was good to see Rob and Evelyn," Rose said. "They couldn't stay long and said to say goodbye to you."

"Oh, I didn't see them leave."

"I think Evelyn wanted to run by the cafe and check on things."

"I hope she's checking to make sure she has everything to bake cinnamon rolls for breakfast." Danny's easy grin tweaked her pulse. Again. "That is, if Allison will let me have breakfast there tomorrow."

"Violet, you should go show Danny the office all decorated up." Rose turned to Danny. "She did a wonderful job."

"Love to see it."

"I'll just carry some of this back to the office with me." She grabbed a tray.

"I'll get the cooler." Danny swung the cooler up and followed her toward the office.

"I guess I'll head back to my cottage now," Rose said to George. It had been nice chatting with him, but she was getting tired. They'd been standing outside for a few hours. She'd enjoyed seeing everyone again, but it sounded inviting to sit down and put her feet up.

"Mind if I walk that way with you?"

"Of course not. Seems like we're almost neighbors. Violet said you bought the house next door? I can't see it from my cottage with that row of areca palms between us."

"Oh, is that what they're called?"

"The prior owner put them in quite a few years ago. They were tiny then, but they grew quickly. I enjoyed seeing how much they'd grown every year."

"So you come here every year?"

"I… yes. I did. My husband and I would come for our anniversary."

"Back when it was Murphy's?"

She looked at him, surprised. "Yes."

"I'd been here a few times when it was Murphy's too. Nice to see how Violet has spruced it all up."

He motioned toward her cottage. "Ready?"

"Yes." She headed across the courtyard and he walked by her side.

"But you're here by yourself now?" George asked quietly.

"I am." She paused and turned to him. "My Emmett passed away this past year. I came back here in September—for what would have been our fifty-year anniversary. Then I ended up staying for a few months."

"I'm sorry for your loss. It's difficult that first

year after you lose your spouse. All the firsts. Learning to live alone."

She looked closely at him, at the same sorrow she saw in her own eyes reflected in his. "You lost your wife?"

"It's been almost three years now. I finally sold the house we'd lived in for years. I just couldn't bear living there any longer. Still miss my Becky. But she wouldn't want me to just spend my days moping around. Decided a fresh start in a new place would do me good. I love the beach and remembered enjoying Moonbeam the few times I'd been here. Seemed like as good a place to move to as any."

"Was it hard to make that decision? To sell the house where you spent so many years with her?"

"It was. But it was the right decision."

"I was just back home. At the house I lived in with Emmett. I can't quite decide what to do with it. Whether I should keep it... or sell it. I actually had a realtor come look at it. A few things I need to fix up to put it on the market. But... I'm just not sure."

"I'm sure you'll make the right decision when it's the right time for you. Whether you decide to keep it or not." Understanding filled his eyes.

It was nice to talk to someone who understood this. To know what it felt like. And it wasn't like he was offering her sympathy. She was tired of seeing the sympathy in everyone's eyes. Or pity. Or the guilty look that they were glad it wasn't happening to them. George's eyes just held understanding.

She turned and continued on toward her cottage, with George walking quietly at her side. She reached the porch and climbed the stairs. "Good night, George. It was nice talking to you this evening."

"Anytime. If you need to talk, I've got time to listen." He smiled at her, his blue eyes sparkling with warmth. He turned and disappeared across the beach and behind the line of areca palms.

CHAPTER 16

Despite Violet's protests that he was a guest, Danny helped her clean up all the mess from the happy hour.

"I don't mind. Really. Glad to help." He carried the table to the office as she carted back a huge vase of bougainvillea with bright pink, almost red flowers. They'd added a pop of color to the table.

"The flowers were a nice touch," Danny said as she placed the vase on the counter.

"They should last a few more days. I just love having flowers around me all year round. Florida is my happy place with year-long blooms of one kind or another. I'm still learning what grows well here though."

"I know what you mean. I was used to such

a short flowering season when we lived in Minnesota. It was quite the change when we moved south."

She walked to the doorway and glanced outside. "I think that's everything."

"Appears so." He leaned the table against the wall. "Your decorations do look nice."

"Even if Rob thinks I went overboard?"

"Nope. It looks great."

She reveled in the compliment. "Would you want to sit and have a glass of wine? Or another beer?"

"I could do that. Beer is fine."

She plunged her hands into the icy water in the cooler and pulled out a couple of beers. They took them out onto the porch and settled onto two chairs.

"That's quite a gathering you put on. I think there were more people than last week."

"I think so. The cottages are full and more people from town dropped by."

"I'm even starting to sort out who is who." The warmth of his friendly laugh wrapped around her and she felt like pulling it close around her, tucking her in safely.

"You've sure met a lot of people since you came here." She briefly glanced over at him, then back to concentrate on the bottle she held in her hands.

"I have. And when I go into town, they remember my name and stop me and say hi."

"Friendly town." She looked up at him again. She couldn't help herself.

"Very. Even the Jenkins twins stopped me yesterday. I know they didn't see us when we went to dinner at the cafe, but evidently, they heard about it. And brought up that we had a second date. I tried correcting them." Amusement flickered in his eyes. "But I get the feeling there is no heading those twins off at the pass. They just run with whatever they decide to run with."

"Pretty much." She laughed. "Sorry about that."

He smiled at her, his eyes twinkling with an easy humor that caused her pulse to quicken. "It's okay. I don't mind."

"If they find out we're both at Donna's watching the boat parade, there'll be more talk." She gave him a wry smile.

"I'm man enough to take it." He grinned back at her. "But seriously. What is this boat parade?"

"I don't know. I've never seen it. I hear it's

wonderful though. A bunch of people decorate their boats and start at the big canal basin at one end of the town and follow a route through the canals and out onto the harbor to finish."

"That sounds interesting. I can't wait to see it."

"Me too. Just one more Christmas activity to add to my growing list. I want to go to the baking contest, but I'm not entering." She shook her head. "No one wants to consume my baking. And there's a sandcastle contest. Not sure how that works because I don't think of sandcastles as Christmassy, but there you have it. Moonbeam has a Christmas sandcastle contest."

"Lots of competition in this town."

"Oh, it's always for a good cause. The library. The history museum. Things like that. And there's a toy drive at Jimmy's. They collect toys, then wrap them and donate them."

"Sounds like a big-hearted town."

"It really is. I can't believe how lucky I am to have landed here. Who knew that when I saw the ad that Murphy's resort was for sale, I'd end up buying it and have this life? And Rob met Evelyn because he came here to help me. So much has happened."

"It's almost like Moonbeam called you two here."

"Or fate. Or whatever you want to believe."

"I think most things happen for a reason. We don't always know what that reason is, but looking back on it, we can sometimes figure it out. Sometimes the worst things that happen to us turn into blessings." He took a sip of his beer, his eyes pensive. "Like I thought it was the end of the world when Linda left Allison and me. But now, looking back, I realize it was the best thing. Linda was never cut out to be a mother, and having her there, ignoring Allison all the time, wouldn't have been good for Alli. And then Allison became really close to my mom when I needed help. My mom was such a kind, giving person and Allison learned a lot from her."

"Things do have a way of working out when you need them to, don't they?" She stretched out her legs, staring at the polish on her toes. They needed to be polished again. She tucked them back under the chair. She'd have to do that before tomorrow night.

"I should go. It's getting late and I want to check in with Allison." He rose from the chair, but she'd swear it was reluctantly. Or was that all her imagination?

"Don't forget that package of Evelyn's cookies."

"Oh, I won't. Or she wouldn't let me forget it." He picked up the wrapped bundle of cookies from the side table. "I'll see you tomorrow then."

"Yes, let's all meet up at five here at the office. Sunset is about five-thirty. And I think the boat parade comes by about seven. We can decide to walk over or drive a few cars. It's not too long of a walk."

"Sounds good. I'll see you tomorrow at five." He turned and crossed the courtyard to the pink cottage.

She sat and finished sipping on her beer. Mulling over the day and all that had happened. Aspen's disappointment. Rose's help with setting up the courtyard. Introducing George to everyone. And Danny's eager help hauling everything in from happy hour. And just spending time with Danny. That had been nice.

She resolutely tamped down her eagerness at seeing him tomorrow at the boat parade. It was just a resort owner showing her guests a good time. Showing off the Christmas activities around town. That was all it was. Wasn't it?

She glanced across the courtyard at the soft light filtering out the windows of Danny's cottage, wishing he was still here, sitting beside her, talking to her. Suddenly the porch that she loved to sit on in the evenings, the porch that comforted her and she enjoyed so much—that very porch was filled with emptiness and loneliness. How had she let things change like this? How had this happened so quickly, so unexpectedly?

And most importantly, what was she going to do about it?

CHAPTER 17

D anny was shocked when Allison didn't even get mad when he told her he was coming to watch the boat parade too. Although she did meet up with Emily at the cafe and walked over separately from him. But still, that was a vast improvement over his previous rocky relationship with his daughter.

He met up with Violet, Rose, and George promptly at five and they all decided to walk over to Donna's. He fell into step beside Violet as they followed Rose and George down the sidewalk and wound their way through town.

They got to Donna's house and were ushered through the house and out to the large screened lanai. Evelyn greeted them. "Oh, good. You all made it."

"Couldn't miss this." Didn't want to miss it. Hadn't wanted to miss spending more time with Violet. Though, that thought was a bit terrifying, and he had to remind himself they were just friends. But having a friend in Moonbeam was nice, right?

He mingled with the people gathered, surprised at how many he knew now, although he occasionally got their names mixed up. But he was getting better at sorting everyone out. He glanced over to where Violet was talking to Allison and Emily. Allison looked over at him and smiled. *Smiled.* His heart soared with the possibility that things were going to work out between them.

Rose walked up to him. "I take it that girl over there with Emily is your daughter, Allison?"

"It is."

"Is she enjoying spending the holidays here?"

"I think so. Though I'm never one hundred percent sure what she's thinking. She surprises me." Like that smile she just gave him. "Constantly."

"Emily is a lovely girl. A good friend to make here in Moonbeam."

"She seems to have a good influence over

Allison. At least I hope so. Allison has changed a lot in the time we've been here. Or maybe it's that she's changed back to how she used to be. She went through a rough patch."

"Hopefully it's over now." Rose touched his arm. "And hopefully you can give her a wonderful Christmas here."

"I certainly hope so." He needed to figure out a gift for her. Something special. The thing was, now that he wasn't as close to her as he used to be, he was clueless on what to get her.

Donna called everyone to come get plates and eat, so he met Violet by the long table spread with every imaginable barbecue food. The hot dogs and brats, baked beans, potato salad, a fruit tray, coleslaw, and a huge tray of Evelyn's Christmas cookies. It all was so tempting. He overfilled his plate with a taste of everything. At this rate, he was going to have to get back to the gym and work out.

He and Violet carried their plates over and sat at a table with Rose and George. The four of them dropped into friendly conversation as they ate. Christmas music drifted softly across the lanai. Laughter floated across the canal from other homes lining the water. The sky darkened, but cheerful lanterns illuminated the tables.

Just as they finished eating, music filtered over from the end of the canal and boats came into view. Everyone gathered at the edge of the large patio as the first boat slipped past them, decorated with a large, light-up Rudolph. Then came boats with Santa waving, huge, decorated presents, a sailboat with lights twined up the mast, and so many more cleverly adorned boats. He stood next to Violet and waved at the passing boats as the people on them waved back and called out greetings. Violet's eyes lit up with excitement like a child's on Christmas morning. He had to admit it was unlike anything he'd ever seen before, and he was thoroughly enjoying himself.

Finally, the last boat disappeared down the waterway, and everyone scattered.

"That was wonderful, wasn't it?" Violet turned to him, joy spread across her face. "Magical."

"It was. I'm so glad they invited me to join you."

She glanced at her watch. "I should get back to the cottages though. Make sure everything is okay there."

"I'll walk back with you. Let me just tell Allison. See if she wants to walk back with us."

He walked over to Alli, but she said she'd walk back with Emily and Blake.

He headed back to Violet. Rose and George had joined her. The four of them thanked Donna for having them.

"Of course. I'm glad you could join us. We love to share all our holiday festivities." Donna turned to George. "And welcome to Moonbeam. I hope you'll enjoy living here."

"So far, it's been wonderful. I've met a lot of people, and you're all so welcoming," George answered.

The four of them headed out back to the cottages. They strolled down the sidewalks, the lamps spilling warm light over them as they crossed underneath them. Rose and George walked in front, chatting away like they'd known each other for years. Violet was quiet by his side.

"Everything okay?"

She looked up at him. "Yes, I was just thinking."

"About what?" He swore she was blushing when they crossed under another lamp and she paused.

"Ah… just things. How this Christmas is turning out even better than I expected."

"For me too. Allison is actually talking to me

these days. And I've met lots of wonderful people." Like Violet. She was who he was really talking about. *She* was wonderful. She enchanted him with her laugh, her warm brown eyes lighting up with amusement. The way her hair framed her face, and she was always tucking it back behind one ear. The way she was full of energy and seemed to enjoy every moment of life.

The way she made his pulse race.

He hadn't been expecting this. And it was foolish to start something up with Violet. He knew that. He and Allison would leave for home after the holidays.

No woman had caught his attention in a long time. Not like Violet had. And he wanted to kiss her.

What?

"You're staring at me." Violet's brow wrinkled.

"I was just thinking that—"

"You two coming?" Rose called back to them.

"Sure, on our way." He left his thoughts back behind them as they hurried to catch up to Rose and George. Thoughts he had no business thinking.

They got back to the cottages and Rose and George headed across the courtyard to their places. He stood on the office porch with Violet.

"It was a great night, wasn't it?" Her face still held the look of enchantment he'd seen while she watched the parade. The look that in turn enchanted him.

"It was a *very* great night." He took a step closer, wondering if he had the nerve to kiss her. Or would that ruin the friendship that had developed between them?

She looked up at him, her eyes shining, questioning.

His heart pounded in his chest, and he moved the tiniest bit closer to her. The sweet scent of her perfume—an almost imperceptible lilac scent—hovered around him, luring him, beckoning him. He took a deep breath. "Ah… Violet. I was wondering—"

"Hey, Dad." Allison came walking up to them.

He whirled around, trying to recover himself, caught in a world between kissing Violet and being a father. "Allison."

Thank goodness he hadn't kissed Violet. What if Allison had seen that? What had he been thinking, anyway? Why take a chance on ruining a perfectly good friendship?

He swallowed, collecting himself. "Thanks for walking her home."

"Sure thing, Mr. Parker." Blake and Emily turned and headed out.

"You coming, Dad?" Allison asked as she started across the courtyard toward their cottage.

"Yes, of course." He glanced at Violet and nodded. "Well, good night. I had a good time."

"Me too," she said softly, a slightly bemused expression on her face.

He hurried after his daughter, glad that he hadn't kissed Violet. That Allison hadn't caught them kissing.

Or maybe disappointed Allison had interrupted them. Who knows what would have happened. Would Violet have wanted to kiss him? Didn't matter—he'd lost his chance.

But did he want another chance? That was the question he had no answer for.

CHAPTER 18

Violet sat outside on the porch the next morning, sipping coffee with Rose. She tried to keep herself from constantly looking over at Danny's cottage.

Rose finally set her coffee down and laughed. "Do you think if you keep staring at his cottage, he'll magically appear?"

"What?" she asked innocently but knew she wasn't fooling Rose.

"Danny's cottage. You can't take your eyes off of it."

"I know." She let out a long sigh. "I just... I'm confused about him."

"What's confusing you?"

"Last night. After you and George left. Danny and I were here on the porch. And I felt this connection with him. An electricity between us. He moved close to me and… I swear he was going to kiss me."

"And would that have been a bad thing?" Rose asked.

"Well, he is leaving after the holidays."

"So that means you can't just have some fun with him now? Enjoy being together?"

"No. Yes." She shrugged. "Anyway, Allison interrupted us. If she really was interrupting anything. Maybe I imagined it all, anyway. And I shouldn't get involved with a guest."

"Oh, there's some law against it?" Rose's eyes twinkled with amusement.

She shrugged again, annoyed at herself. "See, I told you I was confused. I… I like him. It's been a long time since I've liked a guy."

"Maybe you should just relax and see what happens."

"Maybe. But this whole thing could just be my imagination."

Rose shook her head. "I don't think so. I saw the way he looked at you last night when we were watching the boat parade. There was interest in his eyes."

"Maybe he was just enjoying himself."

Rose laughed. "You sure have a lot of excuses."

"I just don't want to get my hopes up and find out it's all one-sided. And he's leaving. I should make that my new mantra. Danny is leaving. There's really no point in starting something with him."

"But sometimes our heart doesn't listen to our words." Rose picked up her coffee. "Anyway, at least think about it. Stay open to it. You never know what might happen."

Rob stopped by the cottages late that morning as she was still ruminating over Rose's words.

"Hey, Rob. What brings you by?"

"Can't I just stop by and see my favorite sister?"

"Only sister." She eyed the Christmas lights in the window, wondering if she could fit just one more strand in there.

"Did you have a good time at the boat parade last night?"

She turned to him. "I did. It was wonderful, wasn't it? And it was so nice of Donna and Evelyn to include me."

"And that Danny guy."

"And Rose and George," she quickly added.

"But Danny. You seem to be seeing a lot of him."

"No, I'm not." Okay, she kind of was.

"I saw how you were looking at him." Rob pinned her with a don't-argue-with-me stare.

"I wasn't looking at him in any certain way." But a blush crept across her face and she knew Robbie could see it.

He came over and rested his hand on her shoulder. "Be careful, sis. I don't want you to get hurt. I saw the way you looked at him. And to be honest, the way he looked at you. But you know he heads back to his real life after the holidays, right? How's that going to work out for you?"

She wanted to deny there was anything between her and Danny. Or tell Robbie to mind his own business. Or something. But after last night, she wasn't sure she could convince him. Or herself. She was *almost* positive Danny had been getting ready to kiss her last night.

Or she'd imagined the whole thing...

She shrugged his hand off her shoulder. "You're imagining things, Robbie. There's nothing between Danny and me. I'm just being a good host. He's my guest."

"If you say so." He shrugged. "Just be careful."

"Thanks for the unsolicited advice." It came out more sharply than she intended. Probably because she knew he was right. She should be careful.

Rob lifted his hands up in defeat. "Sorry. I just worry about you."

"I can take care of myself." That also came out more sharply than she intended. She sighed. "I know you're just being a protective big brother. But really, I'll be fine."

Rob nodded and turned to leave, but his last glance back at her didn't look like she'd convinced him. But then, she hadn't asked for his advice, anyway.

Besides, she was probably imagining this whole thing between Danny and her.

Probably.

Maybe.

CHAPTER 19

Aspen came into work, and Violet headed over to Danny's cottage. Not because she wanted to see him or anything. Or see if she still felt that connection with him. She just wanted to know if he'd like a tree for the cottage. He and Allison really should have one. You needed a tree for a proper Christmas, as far as she was concerned.

Danny answered the door at her knock. A wide smile spread across his face. "Violet, hi."

"Hi, Danny." Was he happy to see her? Was that what his smile said? Though he was naturally a friendly person, so it might not mean anything.

"Come in." He motioned her inside.

Allison sat at the table with work spread before her on the table. "Hi, Violet."

"Hi, Allison."

"I just finished up my last assignment. I'm a free woman for the rest of the holidays."

"Well, that's something to celebrate. How about we go into town and get a Christmas tree for the cottage? Won't that make it feel more like Christmas in here?"

"But we don't have lights or ornaments or anything." Danny's brow creased.

"I have some extra lights. You'll save me from stringing up yet more of them in the office." She grinned.

"Can we, Dad? Please. We could pop popcorn and string it for decorations."

"Okay, sure. It sounds like a great idea," he agreed.

"And I thought we could pick one up for Rose. Surprise her with it. I just want everyone to have a festive holiday."

"Sounds like a plan. We'll take my truck."

And just like that, they were headed to the tree lot beside Parker's General Store. Allison jumped out. "I'm going to find us the perfect tree. This is going to be so great."

She and Danny got out, and he turned to

her. "Thank you for this. Allison is really excited about it. Our Christmas last year was… bleak. I want her to have a wonderful Christmas this year and this will help."

"Sure." She stared into his eyes, trying to decipher the emotion in them. Maybe it was just interest in getting a tree, not in her.

Her thoughts were driving her nuts.

"I should go find Allison."

She nodded and followed after him, staring at his broad shoulders and his long strides.

"Which one do you like?" Allison asked, standing between two trees.

"Your pick, honey." Danny smiled indulgently at his daughter.

She was glad that Danny and Allison were getting along better. This Allison was sure different from the sulking teen who had arrived at the cottages not so long ago.

"Okay, this one is ours. And that one is for Rose."

They paid for the trees and loaded them into the truck. "Let's go into Parker's and see if they have some ornaments, can we?" Allison stood beside the truck. "Just a few. Please?"

"Sure. Good idea."

It appeared that Danny had no willpower to refuse Allison anything she wanted at this stage.

They headed into Parker's and Donna greeted them. "Welcome. Good to see you again."

"We're looking for ornaments. We're going to put a tree at our cottage." Allison's eyes gleamed with anticipation.

"Great idea. Everyone needs a tree for Christmas." Donna pointed across the store. "The Christmas things are over that way and there are more upstairs in our seasonal room."

Allison disappeared, off on her quest for decorations. She returned with her arms laden with everything Christmas and Emily in tow. "Look, I ran into Emily. Can she come help us decorate?"

"Of course."

"And I got some needles and thread to string the popcorn."

Danny paid for Allison's haul and they all headed back to the cottages in his truck.

They set the tree up in front of the window, and Allison and Emily kept spinning it around, trying to find its best side. Danny popped some popcorn in the microwave while Violet helped the girls put the lights on the tree.

Allison and Emily sat down to string the popcorn. "Dad, why don't you bring Rose's tree to her?"

"Good idea."

Violet and Danny rescued the second tree from the truck and carried it between them to Rose's cottage. She knocked at the door, and Rose opened it.

"Surprise. A tree for your cottage."

Rose's eyes lit up, and she clasped her hands together in delight. "Really?"

"Really. And I have more lights, too."

Rose laughed. "Of course you do."

Just then, George came walking up. "Well, hello. I was just coming to see if Rose wanted to take a beach walk."

"How about you stay and help me decorate the tree? Then we can reward ourselves with that walk on the beach."

"Sound like a plan to me."

Danny and George set up the tree, and she handed the lights to Rose. "You should be all set."

"Do you want to stay and help decorate? I have those ornaments that I brought with me."

"I should get back and help Allison with our tree," Danny said.

"And I need to get back to the front desk and give Aspen a break. I could come back later though."

"I'll help her," George said. "We'll get the lights strung and the ornaments hung."

"Okay, thanks, George."

Rose gave her a big hug. "Thank you so much for this. It was so thoughtful."

"You know me and my theory. A person can never have too many Christmas decorations."

Rose laughed. "That does appear to be your motto."

She and Danny headed out as George started stringing the lights on Rose's tree.

"He's a nice man, isn't he?" Violet glanced back at Rose's cottage.

"George? Seems so."

"And it's nice that he and Rose have struck up a friendship. I think she needs company this holiday season. This first one without her husband has to be hard."

"I'm sure it is." They reached the porch of the pink cottage. He turned to her. "I should go in."

"Right, and I have work to do." She started to turn away, and he gently caught her arm. She looked up at him.

"I know we just spent last night at the boat parade. And this afternoon picking out the Christmas trees. But I was wondering if you'd… if you'd like to go out to grab dinner tonight? Allison and Emily are headed into work at the cafe soon."

"I guess it gets old eating alone with Allison working so much."

"It's not that… I just would like to… spend time with you." His eyes shone with hope and something else and held her in their spell. "Violet?"

Had she not answered him? Well, that was his fault. He was the one casting spells over her. "I'd like that, but I can't. I'm working the front desk this evening."

Disappointment clouded his eyes. "I understand."

"But… you could come over to the office later. Maybe we could have a drink together on the porch. Looks like it's going to be nice weather."

His eyes filled with eagerness. "Great. When should I come over?"

"Maybe about six? And then I'll be there at the office if anyone needs anything."

"Perfect. I'll bring a bottle of wine?"

She nodded, unable to speak. There was interest in his eyes. There was no way she could deny it now.

He slipped into the cottage, and she headed over to the office. Drinks with Danny. Spending time with him again. Rob wouldn't be pleased.

But she sure was.

CHAPTER 20

Danny paced the cottage after Allison and Emily left to go work at the cafe. He stopped in front of the tree they'd decorated. It lit up the room with holiday cheer. Strings of popcorn wove their way through the branches. The silver and gold ornaments Allison picked out added to the merriment. Guilt washed over him that he hadn't even gotten a tree for Alli last year. It had just been so hard after his mother died. His heart squeezed just thinking about another Christmas without his mother. He tried to act so strong for Allison, but he missed his mom every single day. He knew Alli did too. But maybe this year they'd figure out a way to celebrate, even with her gone. The tree was a good start.

He walked over and looked out into the courtyard. Maybe if it was all right with Violet, he'd get a strand or two of lights and string them along the porch railing.

Now if he could only think of the perfect gift for Allison. And maybe he should pick something up for Violet too. They had become friends. Nothing big, just a little something. But he had no idea for that gift either. No, maybe they weren't really at a gift-giving stage. He really had no idea what stage they were at.

He puttered around the cottage, glancing at his watch as the minutes just crept by, waiting for six o'clock so he could head over to the office. He chose a nice bottle of red wine he'd picked up and opened it to let it breathe. Then inspiration struck, and he decided to slice up a couple of apples and a block of cheese he had in the fridge. He put them on a plate along with a handful of crackers.

At precisely six, he headed across the courtyard. Violet stood in the doorway to the office and waved to him. He got to the porch and realized he'd forgotten to bring wine glasses.

"I brought this, but forgot glasses."

"Oh, this is nice. Thank you. Appetizers to

go with the wine. Perfect. Let me go grab glasses."

He placed the plate on the table between two chairs, then set the wine down. He sat in a chair but then got right back up. He should wait for Violet. He leaned nonchalantly—hopefully—against the railing, unsure why he was so nervous.

She returned with two glasses and sat on one of the chairs—the one he'd been sitting in—so he took the other one. He poured them wine and lifted his glass. "To new friends."

"New friends." She clinked her glass against his.

New friends? Now why had he said that? But they were friends. She felt like a friend, even if he'd only known her a little while. But couldn't he have come up with a better toast?

"Oh, this wine is delicious." Violet leaned back in her chair, stretching her legs out on the worn deck planks and kicking off her sandals. "The perfect ending to a really nice day."

"It was a nice day. I had a good time getting the trees."

"I did, too. And Rose was so excited to have a tree for her cottage."

"I was going to ask you. Would you mind if

I got some lights and put them up on the railings on our porch?"

She set her glass down, her eyes sparkling with enthusiasm. "Oh, that's a great idea. I'll get lights for each cottage. Won't that make the courtyard look so nice, twinkling lights on each porch? I could put them on timers. What a great idea."

"I'll help you with that." Because it was another excuse to spend time with her.

"Great. I'll pick up the lights at Parker's. Maybe we can put them up tomorrow afternoon?"

"Works for me."

"Of course if Robbie comes to happy hour next Friday and sees them, he'll just say I've gone way over the top."

"As a friend of mine says, you can never have too many Christmas decorations." He winked at her.

She threw back her head and laughed, her eyes sparkling with humor. "A friend, huh?" She laughed again. An infectious sound that made him want to hear it again and again. Watch her eyes light up. Hear her enchanting laugh.

She lifted her glass again, and he tried not to stare at her lips as she sipped her wine. She looked over at him and he gave her a weak grin, trying hard not to spill his own wine. She unsettled him. Made him feel a bit off-kilter. More than a bit.

Like some kind of clueless teenage boy with a crush.

But maybe that was because he couldn't really sort out his feelings for her. Or maybe it was just that he wouldn't admit his feelings for her. Because if he was being honest with himself, he did have feelings for her. Which was silly, of course, because he hadn't known her long. Maybe she didn't want anything more than friendship. Maybe she was more practical than he was and knew it was kind of foolish to start up something that couldn't ever go anywhere. He was leaving. She lived here and ran the resort.

How had all of this gotten so complicated? Or was it just complicated in his mind and there was really nothing more than friendship here? He had no idea.

He was that clueless teenager.

How had everything gotten so complicated in her life? Since when was having a drink on the porch such a bewildering experience?

Violet tried to keep from staring over at Danny. She concentrated on the rim of her glass. Was there a tiny chip on the rim? She twirled it this way and that. No, it was just the way the Christmas lights lining the porch were reflecting on the glass.

She glanced over again and swore she saw something in his eyes. The same look she'd seen last night when she thought he might kiss her.

But then maybe not.

She set the glass down a little more abruptly than she meant, and a few drops splashed out onto the table. She swiped it with her hand.

Danny frowned. "You okay?"

"Yes." She swiped at the drops again. "No."

"What's wrong?" His eyes clouded.

"I'm sitting here with my thoughts ratcheting around at a hundred miles an hour." She paused, wondering if she had the nerve to continue.

He set his drink down. "Mine are too, if that's any consolation."

She stared at him. "They are?"

He nodded, and that look in his eyes got more intense.

"Okay, I'm just going to ask it." She took a deep breath. "Were you getting ready to kiss me last night? Here on the porch. Before Allison interrupted us. Or did I just imagine it?" The words came out in a rush and she held her breath, waiting for his answer. Wondering if she was a fool.

His eyes widened in surprise, then darkened with a heat, a desire. One that was undeniable. "I was going to kiss you. But I wasn't sure if you'd want me to." His brow creased and he tilted his head, his gaze never leaving her face. "Would you want me to?"

"I—I would."

A slow grin spread across his face and he rose from his chair, holding out a hand for her. She took his strong hand, and he pulled her to her feet. Her pulse roared through her like a hurricane wind. Then he gently pushed her hair away from her face. The brush of his fingertips made her catch what was left of her breath.

He locked his gaze with hers as her heart pounded, and she wasn't sure she'd ever breathe again as time stood still.

Excitement and pleasure swept through her

as he leaned down. An electricity jolted her at the touch of his lips. Gentle. Questioning. Then with a bit more intensity. When he finally pulled away, she realized she was grasping his arms for support.

"Ah… that was nice." He ran his finger along her jawline. "Very nice."

She nodded, unable to speak.

As if on cue, Allison came around the corner of the office. "Oh, hi Dad." Then she paused, looked at both of them, and quickly hid a grin.

Violet snatched her hands away from Danny's arms.

"Um, I got off early. We weren't very busy tonight."

"Okay. Good," Danny said as a guilty look crept across his face.

And just like that, the spell was broken. She sank back down into her chair.

"We were just having a drink." Danny stepped back.

"Well, go ahead and finish. I'm going to go read that book you got for me now that my schoolwork is done. See you in a bit."

Allison headed across the courtyard, took

one last look back at them, then disappeared into the pink cottage.

"My daughter has… unusual timing." He gave her a wry grin and sat down again.

"Do you think she saw us kiss?"

"I'm not sure, but I'm certain she knew that something was going on."

"I'm sorry." Guilt mixed with the heady feeling she'd experienced with their kiss swirled through her.

"Don't be sorry," he said softly. "I'm not."

They sat quietly, finishing their drinks, while her thoughts continued to race through her mind.

He finally set down his glass. "I… I don't know where this is headed. I know I'm just a guest here. But I'd like to spend more time with you."

"I'd like that too." *And Robbie would so disagree with that decision.*

"I like you, Violet."

She let those words wash over her, surround her, comfort her, excite her.

"I enjoy spending time with you." She let out a sigh. "What I mean is… I like you too. It's been a long time since… I've liked anyone. Well, you know, a guy." She sounded like a fool.

"It's been a long time for me too. And this has come as quite the surprise to me." He stood and pulled her back up. "And maybe it's foolish since I'm leaving, but I can't seem to stop myself. Don't want to stop myself."

"We could just take it day by day."

He ran his thumb along her cheek, swept her hair back, the whole time staring straight into her eyes. "But I don't want to hurt you. You know, when we leave. And Alli and I do have to leave. Get back to our real lives."

"This feels pretty real to me," she whispered.

"It does." And he kissed her again. And yet again. Then he wrapped his arms around her, holding her close. She could feel his heart beating against her cheek. She let herself get lost in the feeling of his embrace.

Eventually, he dropped his arms and stepped back. "I should go. Check on Allison."

She nodded, the words not coming. She wanted those arms back around her, holding her. Wanted him to kiss her again.

"Good night, Violet." He gave her one last long gaze, his eyes still bright with desire, and turned to cross back to his cottage.

She stood there long after he'd gone inside, staring out into the courtyard. She finally sat back down and picked up her glass, pouring herself more wine. A light breeze ruffled the palm fronds. The scent of the flowers wafted over to her. A seagull called in the distance. The stars twinkled overhead. Was that the Big Dipper? Was it always right up there? How had she not noticed that? The tiny details seemed sharper now.

Things were more complicated now, too. But she wouldn't change that. They'd just have to sort it out. Or maybe just have these next few weeks together, enjoying each other's company. A memory to keep and take out to remember on a long, lonely night.

Because he was right. He had to get back home, and she belonged here in Moonbeam. Here at her beloved Blue Heron Cottages.

But her heart couldn't help leaping with every thought of Danny. The Christmas season that she was already so excited about suddenly got even more thrilling. And she couldn't help but wonder when Danny would kiss her again.

CHAPTER 21

Rose sat on the beach the next morning, enjoying the sunrise. Not many people were out this early, and she enjoyed the quietude. The lone blue heron who often kept her company did not disappoint this morning as he waded along the shoreline. A jogger went past, and an older woman with a bucket, collecting shells.

Older woman. Rose laughed at herself. That woman was probably younger than she was.

"Am I interrupting?" George walked up to her. "I came out to see the sunrise and saw you sitting out here on the beach."

"Not interrupting at all. Want to join me?"

He dropped down on the sand beside her. "Don't mind if I do."

"I really appreciate you helping me decorate the tree yesterday. It was so nice to have it all decorated and lit up last night. Makes it feel more like Christmas."

"It does, doesn't it? I haven't unpacked much at my home, but I do have a tree up. One of the first things I did. Though I haven't found all the ornaments. They're in a box somewhere."

"You haven't finished unpacking?"

"Not everything. It's a bit of an overwhelming job, I admit. My wife was the one who organized the house. Put things in logical places. And the three times we moved, Becky did all the unpacking while I did all the hauling of the boxes." He sent her a small, wry grin. "I'm a bit out of my element, but I'll get there. I'm paralyzed with indecision on where to put things."

"I could come over and help you."

"I couldn't ask that."

"But I offered. Let's just say it's payment for your help with my tree."

He held up his hands. "Okay, you win. I'm not going to turn down your help. Because without it, I'm afraid that six months from now I'm still going to be living among the boxes."

"Great. I'll come over this afternoon. Maybe we'll even find that last box of ornaments and finish up the tree."

"That would be nice."

Rose looked at her watch. "I guess I should get going. I'm having coffee with Violet this morning." She laughed. "Well, I do almost every morning. Watching the sunrise, then coffee with a good friend, is a wonderful way to start the day."

"It sounds like it." George rose and held out a hand for her.

She grasped his hand as he helped her up. His hand felt foreign. Not Emmett's. She shook her head. What a silly thought.

She chased the thought away. "Well, I'll see you this afternoon then."

"This afternoon." George stood there as she walked away.

She crossed the courtyard and headed to the office. Helping George unpack his home would give her a project. A purpose. It would keep her busy. Which was exactly what she needed to get through this first holiday season without Emmett.

Violet saw Rose coming across the courtyard, poured two cups of coffee, and met her out on the porch. "Good morning." She handed the cup to Rose. "Good sunrise?"

"It was. Ran into George," Rose said as she sat down. "I guess he hasn't unpacked much since he moved here. I offered to help him this afternoon."

"That was nice of you. Unpacking can get a bit overwhelming." Violet shrugged sheepishly. "I still have a closet of unpacked boxes. I'm always just so busy with the cottages that I haven't made time to sort through them."

"Maybe you need my help too. I like keeping busy. Especially..." She paused, her eyes filling with sadness.

"This Christmas season, right?" Her heart hurt for Rose and her loss and her pain.

"Yes, Christmas is especially hard. But I'm getting through it. And the tree was such a lovely gift. It really brightens up my cottage." Rose struggled with a weak smile.

"I'm glad you enjoyed it. I wasn't sure if it was too much and you just needed... well... a bit less this Christmas."

"No, it was a thoughtful gift. Thank you."

"I'm going to get some more lights today

and Danny is going to help me put them up on the railings of each cottage."

"Oh?" Rose's eyebrows lifted. "When was all this decided?"

"Last night. Danny… uh… I invited him to come over for a drink. I had to watch the office, but it didn't hurt anything to sit outside and invite a friend over. Kind of like the mornings when you come over for coffee."

"But was it the same?" Rose's eyebrow quirked questioningly as she smiled.

"Okay, not exactly. Not unless you're going to kiss me." What she was fairly certain was a silly grin spread across her face.

Rose laughed. "I knew something was going to happen between you two."

"He kissed me. And… and then Allison interrupted us. I think she saw us kissing." She could remember the exact moment. How she'd blushed and hastily sat down.

"Is that a problem?"

"I really have no clue." She shrugged. "I hope not. Because… because I think I like him."

"Of course you do. It's been obvious to me since about the first time I saw you two together."

"But it's complicated."

"It is." Rose nodded. "But sometimes life throws you curves, and you just have to see where that road leads you."

"I guess. But I like being in control. Knowing what is happening when. I'm not a big fan of surprises."

"And this caught you off guard." It was more of a statement than a question.

"It sure did." She snatched her cup of coffee and took a long sip, the warm liquid soothing her throat. If only it could soothe her nerves. She turned to Rose. "And if Robbie finds out about this, he's going to have some pretty strong opinions."

"He might. But he's just looking out for you."

"I can take care of myself," she said more defensively than she meant to. But could she? Could she take care of herself? Or was she setting herself up for heartbreak? But then, she hadn't known him that long. Why was she making such a big deal out of this?

"Twisting thoughts?" Rose asked, an easy smile playing at the corners of her mouth.

"Swirling, twisting, and mangling all together until I don't know what to think."

"You're just going to have to take it day by day and see how it plays out."

"I hate the unknown," she muttered with uneasiness. "Hate it."

"You'll just have to decide for yourself if Danny is worth it. Worth taking a chance and seeing where things go with him."

"I don't think I have a choice." A long sigh escaped her. "I'm pretty sure I've already fallen for him." And she wasn't sure how she felt about that, either. There was just way too much unknown in her life right now.

CHAPTER 22

Danny couldn't help but glance out the window toward the office. Rose and Violet sat on the porch chatting and sipping coffee. He held his own cup and wished he were over there with them. But he didn't want to interrupt their morning ritual. And he hadn't been invited. Besides, he had plans with Violet this afternoon. Decorating all the cottage railings. It wasn't like he could spend *all* his days with her.

Still, he stood at the window, wishing he was across the courtyard. He shook his head and moved away, sitting down at the table. He really should get some work done.

The coffee pot was empty by the time Allison woke up.

"Morning." Sleepiness clung to the word.

"Stayed up late?"

"I did. That book you got me was so good. I kept telling myself just one more page. But I didn't listen." She shook her head. "I still didn't finish it."

"I'm glad you're enjoying it." It had been a long time since he'd seen her reading.

As if she could read his mind, she said, "I love reading. I don't know why it's been so long since I've picked up a novel. If I finish this one, can we go to the bookstore and get another one?"

"Of course." He would never deny her another book. He could hardly ever deny her anything. Especially since she seemed so happy now.

She poured herself a glass of orange juice, and he congratulated himself again for having a healthy choice for her. That's what fathers did, right? Although his mother had done the grocery shopping for all of them for years. He hadn't done a very good job of it since she'd passed away. They ate a lot of frozen pizza and junk food. But that was going to change.

She sat down across from him and he closed his laptop, unwilling to miss a moment of this time with his daughter. The one who had just sat down across from him instead of skulking off, ignoring him.

She leaned back in her chair and set the glass down. "So… you and Violet."

So she had seen them. He wasn't sure what to say. He finally simply came up with, "I… I like her."

"Well, duh, Dad. I've known that for quite a while."

"You have?" He stared at her in surprise.

"Of course." She shrugged. "And Violet is cool."

"She is. Very cool." And fun. And pretty. And charming. And so many other things.

"So, you're going to date her while we're here?"

"I am." He hesitated, then plunged on. "You're okay with that?"

"Pretty sure you don't need my permission to date someone," she said wryly.

"I know. But I just want to make sure——"

She held up a hand. "Dad. It's fine. Really."

Relief spilled through him. Allison was right. He didn't need her permission to date anyone, but he was glad she was okay with him seeing Violet.

Allison leaned forward. "Oh, and I'm entering the cookie contest. I'm going to use Gran's spice cookie recipe. Evelyn said I could use the kitchen at the cafe, but we'll have to get the ingredients."

His mouth dropped open in amazement. Just how many times could she surprise him this morning? "You are?" He tried to recover. "Well, that's great. I'll take you grocery shopping whenever you want."

"Thanks, Dad."

He tried to hide his surprise and act like a normal father. "So are we still on for going on The Destiny tomorrow evening?"

"Yes, it will be fun. And hey, why don't you ask Violet to join us?" She grinned at him.

So she must be really okay with his seeing Violet. And asking her to go with them... what a great idea. Another chance to spend time with her.

Allison pushed off the chair. "I've got to go get ready. I've got a shift at the cafe."

"You're sure working a lot. You okay with that?"

"I like working there. I've met a ton of people. And they have regulars who come in and I'm learning their names. They know me and my name. It's kind of cool."

"It's a friendly town, isn't it?"

"It is. I feel like I've made more friends here than I have back home. And Emily was the one who suggested I enter the contest when I was telling her about how Gran and I used to bake all the time."

And her friends here were the kind of friends he wanted her to have. Ones who didn't go out drinking and causing trouble. Ones who actually went to class and got good grades.

"I'm glad you're enjoying our time here."

"I am." She got up and set her glass in the sink. "I'm really going to miss it when we leave." She disappeared down the hallway.

He rose and wandered over to the window and looked across to the office porch. It was empty now. He walked back and sat down, opening his laptop. But he couldn't concentrate on the work.

Allison's words still swirled around him. He was going to miss Moonbeam when they left, too. And Violet.

He slid his fingers through his hair, wondering if he needed a haircut. He could ask

Violet to recommend someone… Or was that just an excuse to see her?

What had he gotten himself into? And Allison, for that matter. She'd made good friends here. Emily and her group of friends had accepted her and included her. She was entering the town's cookie-baking contest, for Pete's sake. A month ago, he would have never believed all this could happen.

But really, none of that mattered. Well, it mattered, but they still had to leave after the holidays. He'd just have to concentrate on making sure Allison had the best Christmas he could possibly give her.

And suddenly he knew the perfect gift for her. A grin crept across his face. The *perfect* gift. He was certain this new version of Alli would love it.

Walker stood in his office at Jimmy's and shook hands with Mr. Shelton. "Thanks so much. I really appreciate it."

"My pleasure." Mr. Shelton headed out of the office.

Walker stared at the package in his hand, a

smile creeping over his face. Everything was working out perfectly. As he moved over to the desk and opened the drawer, Tara came rushing in.

"I think Aspen saw Mr. Shelton."

"Did she see he was here in the office with me?"

"No, I don't think so. She came in early for her shift. Hopefully she just thinks he finished up eating here."

"I hope so."

"Hi, Walker." Aspen appeared in the doorway behind Tara.

She startled him so badly he nearly jumped out of his skin. He glanced around the room, wishing he could hide.

"What are you two up to?"

"Up to? Nothing." Guilt crept through him.

"Oh, I thought—never mind." She looked at him closely as if waiting for him to do… something. The three of them stood awkwardly in the room. Finally, Aspen spoke. "Well, I guess I should get to work." She turned and left after giving him one more questioning glance.

"That didn't go well. Why didn't you at least go over and kiss her hello?" Tara frowned at him.

He held out his hand. "Because I was holding the ring box."

Tara shook her head. "Hide that thing and get yourself out there and find her. She looked hurt."

"I know. She just caught me by surprise." He dropped the box in the desk drawer and locked it. "I'll go catch up with her."

"Good plan. I can't wait until this is all over."

"Me too. I feel guilty keeping secrets from her, but I want to surprise her at Christmas."

"Then get out there and act normal." Tara shook her head. "At least as normal as you ever are."

"Ha, ha, sis." He brushed past her and headed out to track down Aspen and make amends. But it all would be worth it in the end. At least he hoped so.

CHAPTER 23

When Aspen came into the office after her breakfast shift at Jimmy's, Violet could feel her anxious energy. "Are you okay?"

"Yes." Aspen came behind the desk, then sighed. "No. Oh, I don't know."

"What's wrong?"

"It's Walker. He's acting… strange."

"How so?"

"Secretive. And he didn't even kiss me hello this morning. He… he always kisses me hello. Always used to tell me he missed me terribly even if I just saw him the night before. I'm afraid… I'm afraid he's losing interest in me."

"That's silly. Of course, he's not."

"I don't know. And he's always whispering with Tara. Like he's hiding something." Aspen frowned. "Do you... do you think he's seeing someone else?"

Violet shook her head. "In this town? How would he keep that a secret around here?" She gave a little laugh. "For sure the Jenkins twins would find out."

"You're probably right. But I know something is going on."

"Maybe it's about a Christmas gift."

"Maybe. But it feels like it's more than that." Aspen sighed. "Anyway, I'll take over here so you can decorate the railings. I think that's a great idea, by the way. We're going to have the most festive place in Moonbeam."

"That's my plan." She grabbed a bag full of Christmas lights. "Danny's going to help me put them up."

The worry lines vanished from Aspen's forehead as she grinned. "Of course he is."

"He's just being helpful," she protested. But it even sounded weak to her ears.

"Whatever you say." Aspen bit her lip, struggling to smother another grin.

Violet ignored Aspen and her grins and walked out into the sunshine. Danny sat on his porch. When he saw her, he got up and jogged across the courtyard.

"I'm at your service." He gave her an exaggerated bow.

Her heart fluttered in her chest. "I have the lights." *Way to go, Violet. State the obvious.*

But she couldn't stop staring at his lips. The memory of his kisses trampled to the front of her mind, stomping out any rational words or thoughts.

He glanced around the courtyard, then looked at her. "Looks like no one's outside. Think I could steal a quick kiss?"

Her pulse sped up as she looked around. No one. She nodded, holding her breath, waiting for the feel of his lips on hers.

He kissed her quickly, then swept his gaze around the courtyard again. Then kissed her one more time, this time lingering before pulling away.

"We probably should get started," he said as he stepped back.

"What?" She stared at him. All she could see was him. The whole world had faded away.

"The lights? We should get started on the lights." An irresistible, slightly amused grin slipped across his lips. The lips she'd just kissed. "Violet?"

"Right. The lights." She better pull herself

together. She was acting like a fool. A fool who had fallen in love.

What?

Where had that come from? Who said anything about love? She just liked him. Enjoyed spending time with him.

Just keep trying to convince yourself of that.

Danny couldn't keep from staring at Violet as they strung the lights on the porches. Their hands brushed—many times—as they wound the lights around the railings. He worked closer to her than necessary but he just couldn't make himself step back and give her space. He liked being near her.

Regretfully, they finally finished the last porch. "I can't wait to see them all lit up this evening." Violet's eyes shone with excitement.

"I'm sure it will look magical."

"I really appreciate your help with all of this."

"It was no problem." There wasn't any place he'd rather be. "Oh, I meant to ask you. I'm taking Allison on The Destiny tomorrow night. Would you like to join us?"

"Are you sure?"

"I'm sure. It actually was Alli's suggestion."

"Okay, that sounds like fun. I'd love to go with you."

Excitement and eagerness bubbled through him. He'd get to see Violet again tomorrow. Tomorrow. *Tomorrow*. It sing-songed through his mind.

She took one last look around at the cottages. "I should probably get back to the office. Have some paperwork to do."

"Right. I have some work to do too." If he could force himself to concentrate on anything other than Violet, which was getting increasingly harder to do with each passing day.

She stood there, not leaving. He took a quick step toward her and grasped her hand, pulling her closer. "One kiss to tide me over?" He gave her his best impish grin to entice her.

"You know, you don't really have to flash me that wheedling grin. I'm pretty much a sure thing." She stood on tiptoe and kissed him. "Will that work?"

"For a while." He stepped back, still holding her hand.

"I should really go." She glanced down at their hands.

"You should."

She slowly slid her hand from his. "I'll see you later?"

"You sure will."

She crossed over to the office and gave him a small wave before disappearing inside. The courtyard was suddenly achingly empty.

Allison was thrilled about how well the dinner shift was going. She was really getting the hang of working here. Knew most of the menu by heart. Even when they got busy, she no longer got flustered. As the rush died down, she cleared a table, hauled the dishes back to the kitchen, and set them by the dishwasher.

Emily walked in with another tray of dishes. "Looks like the rush is over."

"It does."

"Want to sit and have a piece of pie? Evelyn made peach today."

"I do."

They grabbed slices of pie and went out and sat at the counter so they could watch in case anyone else came in.

"Evelyn is like the best baker in the world.

This crust is to die for." Allison took another bite. "Truly. Flaky and almost melts in your mouth."

"She is."

"Does she enter the cookie baking contest? I'd never beat her, even with Gran's recipe."

"She usually does, but she said she's too busy this year to enter." Emily laughed. "So at least you have a fighting chance."

She didn't really care if she won or not. She just wanted to feel a part of it all. A part of Moonbeam. To feel like she belonged. Even though she didn't, really. She was just a visitor.

"So, I was doing some more research on the Parkers. I'm a bit stuck a couple of generations back though. I'm going to talk to my great-grandmother, Patricia. She might know more. She's out of town right now, but she'll be back by Christmas. And I found some photos, but they aren't labeled or anything, so I don't know who they are. But I'd like to get things a little more definite before I finish up my paper on the town's history. And my boss at the history museum wants me to put a copy of my paper in the museum."

"That's pretty cool."

"Yeah, it is. I'm pretty much enamored with

history." Emily paused with a rueful shake of her head. "Too bad there isn't much of a way to make a living just researching history. But I do plan on taking all the history electives I can when I go to college."

College. There it was again. Emily with her plans and dreams. "I've been thinking I should maybe start looking into colleges," Allison admitted. "That is if I can fix my grades. I really messed up this year and let them slide."

"I bet you can bring them up. It will probably just take a lot of hard work. Maybe ask the teachers for extra credit work."

"I was just so… foolish… this last year or so. I let this group of friends influence me. And not in a good way."

"Hey, we all make mistakes." Emily's eyes held no judgment.

"And I was such a brat to my dad. And he's been nothing but wonderful to me my whole life. Always there for me. But after Gran died… I just… Well, it was hard."

"I bet it was. I can't imagine losing my grandmother."

"But I shouldn't have let it just implode my life. I'm going to do better."

"If you want help on that college search, I'll

work with you. And even after you leave, we can text and video chat."

"I'd love that." Nice to keep in touch. Though she knew that as time went on and she was away, they'd drift apart. That was how it worked. She rarely spoke to her friends she'd had in Atlanta before they moved to Tallahassee. "I'll miss you when we leave," she admitted.

"Hey, I'll miss you too. It's been great having you here. I like that we became friends."

She'd just have to find new friends when she went back home. Avoid the old group. And if she couldn't make new friends, she'd just deal with being without them until she graduated. She could do that.

Just then, Blake came hurrying into the cafe and slid onto a stool beside them. "Hey, I just talked to my dad. Allison, he said your dad just made reservations for The Destiny tomorrow for three."

"He was going to invite Violet to go with us. I guess she said yes."

"I'm working on the Destiny tomorrow. You should come, too, Emily. It would be fun."

"Yes, Emily. Can you come?" It would be

great to have even more time with her friends before she had to go back home.

"Sure. That does sound fun."

"Perfect. I'll tell Dad. I'll be busy working, but I should have some time to hang out with you guys." Blake got up. "I can't stand it. I'm going to go grab a piece of that peach pie."

A customer came in and Allison jumped up. "I'll get them. You finish your pie." She hurried over to greet the customer—she knew his name, Mr. Poplar—and seated him at a table by the window.

Another couple came in and Emily went to help them, and suddenly they had a flood of late diners. But she didn't mind. She liked it when they were busy at the cafe. And she liked that she could keep up with Emily serving the customers.

She liked just about everything about Moonbeam except... the fact they would have to leave.

CHAPTER 24

They all boarded The Destiny about thirty minutes before departure. The main area of the boat was decorated with Christmas lights and a tree in the corner secured to a nearby railing.

Allison and Emily went off to find Blake, and Violet followed Danny up to the upper deck. Christmas lights and bright red bows were hung on the railing, lending a cheerful and festive look to the deck. They stood along the railing, watching people board. A few other boats at the marina headed out into the harbor to catch the sunset.

Danny's arm brushed hers, and Violet reveled in the feeling of him standing next to her. She had to admit that she was hoping he'd sneak a quick kiss. But that probably wouldn't happen with Allison and Emily onboard.

He smiled down at her and covered her hand, resting on the railing. "This is nice, isn't it?"

"It is. And it looks like we might have a wonderful sunset tonight."

"I ordered it up special for us." His eyes twinkled.

"That was good of you." She grinned back at him. "Thoughtful."

"I'm a thoughtful kind of guy."

Allison and Emily came out on the upper deck. "Found Blake. He's going to join us up here after we launch." Allison came over and stood beside Danny.

He didn't take his hand away from hers. And she wasn't sure if she should pull back or how she felt about it. How Allison felt about it.

She looked up at Danny, and he winked at her. Okay, things must be okay with Allison knowing about them.

They stood at the railing as The Destiny maneuvered out of the marina and headed out across the harbor. They'd make it to the gulf before sunset. The Destiny slid through the water and headed west.

Emily and Allison left to go explore around the boat. She and Danny stayed by the railing, watching the water slip past and birds fly overhead. She pointed out some of the huge homes lining the harbor. "They sell for in the millions. I can't imagine having that kind of money. And some of those houses sit empty except for when the snowbirds come down in January through about the end of March. All that real estate just sitting empty."

"I guess you get pretty busy during that time of year too, don't you?"

"I'm almost booked for the winter. I even have a couple of month-long rentals. I have to admit, I was relieved when I saw the reservations pouring in. Then there's Rose, of course. Not sure how long she's staying. I'm not going to book anyone in her cottage until she knows how long she's staying. She said at least through January."

"I wish Allison and I could stay longer. It's going to be hard to leave Moonbeam." He stared at her for a moment. "Leave you."

She swallowed. It would be hard when he left. She was getting used to spending time with him. Talking to him. He made her laugh, and she looked forward to every minute they had together.

He glanced around, then leaned over and kissed her quickly. Just a hint of heat on her lips. Then he pulled away. "Hopefully, when we get back to the cottages, I'll be able to do that properly."

She nodded. How could one quick kiss make her thoughts bounce around so she could barely speak?

The Destiny slipped out into the gulf, the water turning turquoise as they left the harbor behind them. They stood in silence as the sky splashed a brilliant display of oranges and yellows across the sky as the sun slipped down beneath the horizon.

"That was magical," she whispered. So much more so to be sharing it with Danny.

He squeezed her hand. "It was. I'm glad you came with us."

Allison and Emily walked up. "Dad, we're going downstairs. They put out snacks and soda. You want to come?"

"Sure do." They followed the girls down the stairs to the main room of the boat. A long table stretched across one end, filled with snacks and drinks. They all grabbed something and sat at a table. Blake joined them.

"This is really nice, Blake. I heard your dad remodeled the boat," Violet said.

"He did. That was before I was here. But he's always working on keeping it looking good. The other day when we didn't have a cruise, I helped him re-varnish the railings upstairs. He likes to keep everything in top shape. He's crazy about this boat." Blake grinned. "My mom says she's not sure if he loves her or The Destiny more."

"Heather, of course." Emily laughed. "He's nuts about my aunt."

"Yeah, Mom is pretty great."

"It's that whole Parker women thing. We're all great," Emily teased.

They finished the cruise just sitting and chatting with the kids. She was glad Allison had made friends with Emily and Blake. Allison seemed like a different girl than the one who was so mad to be here in Moonbeam when they arrived. Danny was different now too. More relaxed, without the wariness that hovered in the corners of his eyes when he first got here. Of course back then he was constantly worried about Allison and struggling to get her to even speak to him. How things had changed.

But Moonbeam was like that. It had a way of sorting things out for people. And it was the Christmas season. A magical time of the year, full of family and friends.

"What are you thinking?" Danny leaned close, whispering the question.

"That everything is just... perfect."

"I'll have to agree with you on that." He kept his voice low but reached over and squeezed her hand resting on her lap. "Perfect."

And she was just going to enjoy the simple moments like this. Sitting and talking with Danny and the kids. Sharing the sunset. Enjoy all these extraordinary ordinary moments.

When they arrived back at the cottages, Allison turned to him. "Dad, I'm going in to finish my book. But I'm going to make some popcorn. Want some?"

"Sounds good. I'll be over in a minute."

Allison crossed over and disappeared inside their cottage. He turned to Violet. "Now I can have that kiss?" The kiss he'd been wanting all night. The need to feel her in his arms. Hold her for a few moments and let the world just fade away.

He pulled her close, wrapped his arms around her, and leaned down to kiss her. He lingered, enjoying every moment before finally pulling away. Slightly. He didn't want to let her go. A bemused expression settled on Violet's face, and he enjoyed the fact that he'd put it there.

"So I'll see you tomorrow?" He reached out and tucked a lock of her hair behind her ear, pausing to brush her cheek with his finger.

"We have plans?" she asked. And he swore she was staring at his lips.

Which made him kiss her again, of course. What was a man to do? At last he pulled away. "Yes, we have plans. I don't know what they are, but I want to see you tomorrow. Even if we do nothing."

"Nothing sounds good to me."

He reluctantly let her go, his arms achingly empty as he stepped away from her. "I should go to the cottage. Have popcorn with Allison."

Violet nodded. "You should. I had a wonderful time tonight. Thanks for including me."

"Tomorrow then?"

"Tomorrow."

And with her promise that he'd see her tomorrow, he headed across the courtyard. He stood on his porch for a moment, staring back at her on the office porch. They both stood there for a few minutes, watching each other. She finally lifted a hand in a wave and slipped inside.

He stood and glanced up at the stars tossed above in the night sky, watching over them. "Mom, you up there?" he whispered. "I'm trying my best this Christmas. Trying to give Allison a good holiday. And I think that maybe, just maybe, Alli and I are back on good footing. If you helped to nudge her, I appreciate it."

It might be silly to talk to the heavens, talk to his mom like this. But he believed she could hear him.

"Night, Mom." He slipped inside to spend time with his daughter. A wonderful change from just a few weeks ago.

CHAPTER 25

Allison and Emily stood in the kitchen at the cafe the next evening after they closed. Allison was covered in flour from a spillage mishap, and Emily wasn't faring much better.

"It's a lot harder to make such a large batch of these cookies. I'm not sure they're going to turn out right." Allison frowned at the mess they'd made.

"I don't know. This first batch is wonderful." Emily munched on a cookie. "And you haven't even decorated them yet."

"I've got the icing made up. And Gran taught me how pipe the frosting so it looks like snowflakes on the cookies."

"Honestly, we hired you to work the wrong

part of the cafe. You should be here in the kitchen with Evelyn. Baking. These are really great."

After the first batch of cookies cooled, she carefully piped a delicate snowflake design on each one.

She started humming a Christmas carol while they worked. She and Gran always sang Christmas carols while they baked. Before she knew it, she was singing "Deck the Halls," and Emily joined in. Then she started into "Silent Night." Emily stopped singing and stared at her.

Allison stopped after the first verse. "Why are you staring at me?"

"You have a beautiful voice. Really great."

She blushed. "Thank you. I used to sing in the choir. But I dropped out when we moved this last time."

"Well, you're really talented."

"Thanks." She turned back to the cookies, embarrassed at the compliments. "I should finish these up."

It was midnight before they finished and got the kitchen cleaned up. She'd carefully boxed up cookies for the bake sale and arranged a plate of the prettiest ones for the contest.

Just then, her father walked in. "Got your

text. You ready to go home? We'll drop off Emily on the way."

"We're ready. I just have to come back tomorrow and bring these over to City Hall where they have the sale and contest."

"I bet she wins. These cookies are delicious. And she did such a great job of decorating them."

"I don't suppose you saved any for me?" Her dad grinned at her.

"But of course." She handed him a box of cookies.

"You're my favorite daughter."

She rolled her eyes but was glad she'd thought to set some aside for him. "I just bet I am."

They headed out. She was exhausted and exhilarated at the same time. And couldn't wait to see how her cookies fared at the sale and in the contest.

They wound their way through the streets. It was strange to think it was so safe to just walk around at midnight here in town. They definitely wouldn't have been doing that back home. After dropping off Emily, they headed back to their cottage. They walked inside and a feeling of being home swept through her.

More like home than their house back in Tallahassee.

She kissed her father good night. "Thanks, Dad."

"For what?"

"For not listening to me when I refused to come here to Moonbeam. For bringing me anyway. For… for being patient with me this last year or so. I'm really sorry about how I acted. Embarrassed."

He wrapped his arms around her and hugged her. "It's okay. It was a really hard year for you."

She looked up at him. "It was. And I'm really hoping this next one is so much better."

"It will be, Alli. It will be."

CHAPTER 26

The next morning, Danny sat outside drinking his coffee, waiting for Allison to get up so he could drive her to pick up the cookies and deliver them to City Hall. The bake sale and contest were tonight, followed by caroling by the gazebo. He felt like he'd been dropped into the middle of some Christmas movie these days. The small-town charm, the friendly people, all the festivities… and Violet. Falling for Violet. And falling he was. He knew that. He couldn't even try to deny it now.

Violet came out of the office and waved. He waved back, hoping she would come over, but Rose walked out behind her and they settled onto two chairs for their morning coffee.

He finished his coffee and headed back

inside. At least he'd had a glimpse of Violet to start his day.

He took out his laptop and started working. Luckily, work was slow right now, because he was having the worst time concentrating. He mindlessly started cleaning up his inbox with the way too many emails he'd ignored. A knock broke his barely there concentration, and he went to answer the door. Violet stood there smiling, a plate in her hands.

"Hey, Rose brought me some cinnamon rolls from the cafe. I thought I'd share with you and Allison."

His pulse quickened with anticipation. Even though he tried to tell himself it was because of the coveted cinnamon rolls, he knew it was because of Violet. "Come in for a sec?"

"Sure." She stepped inside.

He took the plate of rolls and set it on the table, then crossed quickly back to her side. She smiled up at him, pulled him close, and kissed him. He kissed her back and her arms wrapped around his neck as he pulled her closer.

"Uh... sorry." Allison's voice caught him off guard.

He pulled away from Violet and turned to see Allison standing there grinning. Violet turned bright red, and he was sure he was almost the same color.

"We... uh... need to go get the cookies and get them to City Hall."

"Your dad..." Violet seemed to recover. Slightly anyway. "He said you entered the contest. Good luck."

"Thanks. But I don't really care if I win. It was fun to bake Gran's recipe again. And the bake sale is for a good cause. It just made me feel... feel like part of something special."

"Well, good luck."

"Are you coming tonight to the sale?" Allison asked.

"I am. I'll be there at eight when they announce the winner of the contest." Violet stepped back further from him, her blush lessening somewhat. "I'll see you then."

"Bye, Violet," Allison said as she walked to the fridge to grab some orange juice.

"Here, I'll walk you out." He walked outside with Violet, closing the door behind him.

"I'm so sorry. I shouldn't have kissed you like that. Not in your cottage."

"It was fine. I'm glad you did." He winked at her. "Best way ever to start a day."

"But... Allison."

"She's fine. Really." He gave her a quick kiss. "But I should go back in and get her over to pick up and deliver the cookies. A big day for her. I'll see you tonight at the sale?"

"Wouldn't miss it."

He watched Violet cross the courtyard before he slipped back into the cottage.

Allison swore she'd walked around the bake sale at least a hundred times this evening. Carefully looking at each entry in the contest and critically eyeing the competition. Not everyone who brought cookies for the bake sale had entered the contest, but there were still a lot of entries.

The tables of cookies lined the sidewalks in front of City Hall, with the contest table at the far end of the street near the gazebo.

Emily appeared through the crowd. "Hi. Sorry I'm late. Got tied up at the cafe. Wow, look at all the entries this year."

"Those two ladies... the twin ones... they keep hovering around and talking to the judges." The two, dressed identically, chattered away with the judges. Was that allowed? Should she go over and talk to them? Act friendly?

"That's Jackie and Jillian Jenkins. They entered this year. They enter almost every year. Came into the cafe and announced they were going to win." Emily laughed. "But they won't. Their cookies are... let's just say, they're not known for their baking skills. I bet you'll win."

"But I'm not really even a Moonbeam resident. They should disqualify me." She chewed on her lip.

"Nah, we have people from over on Belle Island enter. Julie from The Sweet Shoppe enters some years. But I don't think she is this year."

People milled about, stocking up on cookies, cheerfully contributing to the bake sale and the causes it supported each year. Nervous energy swept through her. Maybe one more circle along the sidewalk?

Emily tugged on her arm. "Come on. Let's go find Blake. If you just stand here, you're going to chew off your lip."

She let Emily drag her down the sidewalk, away from the long table with the contest entries. She did glance back once though, glad to see the twins move away from the judges.

They walked around without finding Blake and returned to the contest table.

Her dad came walking up to her, and she was comforted by the sight of him. "I'm so glad you made it." He was always there for her. Always. Which made a wave of guilt flush through her at how she'd treated him the last year. She hugged him.

He smiled, surprised, and hugged her back. "Of course I'm here for you. Wouldn't miss it."

"Allison is going to wear out the sidewalks pacing around, waiting for the judging," Emily teased. "The mayor should start it all soon."

Just then, the squeak of a loudspeaker shot across the distance.

"That's the mayor." Emily nodded toward the speaker.

"Welcome to our annual Christmas cookie contest. Looks like we have some wonderful entries this year. Judges, it's time to start." The mayor motioned to the contest table.

Her dad grinned down at her. "Good luck, kiddo. I'm so proud of you for entering. For using Mom's recipe."

"Thanks. I hope I did Gran proud." She turned to watch the judges. One by one, they sampled the cookies, but their expressions gave nothing away. They got to her entry, and she held her breath.

Emily squeezed her arm. "You've got this."

Still, she had no idea how her cookies did. How did those judges keep such somber faces?

After sampling all the cookies, the judges gathered at the far end of the table, their heads together, talking softly. Finally, they all stepped back and nodded. One judge went over and whispered to the mayor.

The mayor stepped up to the microphone again. "May I have your attention? Our judges have done a wonderful job this year. Tough job, sampling all those cookies." He chuckled. "But we have a winner. And the winner is…" He paused, drawing out the suspense.

Her father dropped his arm around her shoulder and smiled encouragingly. She glanced over at the twins, who looked expectantly at the mayor. They might win. Anyone might win. She held her breath, clutching Emily's hand.

"Our winner is… Allison Parker."

She gasped and Emily hugged her so tight she squeezed what little breath she had right out of her.

"Way to go, sweetheart. I'm so proud of you," her dad congratulated her.

"Allison, will you come up here and get your prize?"

Stunned, she wound her way up toward the mayor. He handed her a silver trophy that said First Place, Christmas Cookie Contest. She clutched it close to her heart.

"Thank you."

The crowd burst into applause, and she couldn't keep the goofy grin from spreading across her face. In that moment, she felt a part of the town. Part of the festivities. Part of... Christmas. Tears sprang to the corners of her eyes. If only Gran were here to see this.

She caught her father's look from the distance and his proud smile. She smiled back at him.

She'd won the cookie contest. She'd made her grandmother proud. She glanced up at the sky and lifted the trophy slightly, silently thanking her grandmother for all the years in the kitchen, teaching her to bake.

A small group from the high school band started playing Christmas carols over at the gazebo. The crowd drifted away, buying more cookies, sipping hot chocolate, and wandering over to the gazebo.

Her father and Violet came up to her, and her dad wrapped her in a hug. "I'm so very, very proud of you."

"Thanks, Dad."

"I got here just in time to hear them announce you won. Great job." Violet offered her congratulations.

Tears threatened to overwhelm her again.

"You okay, honey?" Her dad looked closely at her.

"Yes, I'm fine. Just… happy. Really happy. I love it here."

"Me too, Alli. Me too."

They headed over to the gazebo to join the caroling. Danny's heart felt lighter watching as Alli and Emily chattered away until they reached the gazebo, then joined in the singing. He hadn't seen her this happy and content in a very long time.

The heavy burden he'd been carrying the last year—worried about every choice Allison made, every mistake she made, feeling like a failure as a father—started to ease. He felt like dancing or twirling or shouting with joy, like a young boy who'd made his first home run. Instead, he leaned his head near Violet's. "I'm really glad you showed up tonight."

"I wouldn't have missed it. I'm thrilled for Allison."

"I am too. She's a changed person since coming to Moonbeam."

"Moonbeam has a way of doing that to people." The corners of her mouth curved into a gentle smile, and he tried not to stare at her lips.

His attention was broken when the mayor got up to speak after the carol ended.

"I've had a special request from the Parker women. They'd like our cookie contest winner, Allison Parker—no relation to *our* Parkers—to lead us in a carol. How about it, Allison?"

He searched the crowd for Allison and saw her frozen at the edge of the gazebo. Emily grinned and nudged her. Allison stepped forward and climbed the stairs. She went over to the band and talked to them for a moment before coming out to the edge of the gazebo. The band started playing "Silent Night." Allison's voice floated across the distance and tears threatened his eyes as his heart soared. He felt Violet's hand on his arm, but he couldn't tear his eyes from Alli. After the first verse, she motioned the crowd to join in. As everyone's voices mingled with hers, he cleared his throat and started singing. He glanced down at Violet, who smiled with her eyes as she sang along.

Finally, the carol ended, and the crowd grew silent for a moment, then burst into applause. Allison gave a small wave, a wide grin plastered across her face, and hurried off the gazebo and over to Emily's side. They headed over to him and he swooped Alli up in a hug, swinging her around like he'd done when she was a girl.

She laughed. "Dad, put me down."

He did as instructed. "That was beautiful, honey. It's been so long since I heard you sing."

"Yeah, I forgot how much I love it. I think I might see if I can join the choir when we go back home."

Back home. Allison's words broke through his happiness, his contentment, and reminded him they'd soon be leaving. A thought he didn't want to dwell on.

"Emily just texted Blake and we're going to go meet him. Can I just meet you back at the cottage? They'll walk me back to the resort."

"Sure. I'll see you later. Not too late."

Allison nodded, then hurried off with Emily, disappearing into the crowd.

"Now what? Do you want to stay a while?" he asked Violet.

"Let me buy some cookies. I'm going to put them out for happy hour tomorrow."

Soon they were carrying stacks of cookie boxes, and they headed back to the cottages. They got to the office and set all the cookies on the counter in the reception area.

"I guess I should go. It's getting late." And he knew Violet was an early riser.

"I guess you should." She looked up at him, her eyes sparkling, questioning. "But I really don't want you to."

He pulled her into his arms, holding her close. The faint scent of orange blossoms surrounded him as he stroked her hair. "I think I could stand here like this forever," he whispered softly.

She turned her head to look up at him. "I could too. I'm... I'm going to miss you."

He pushed back a lock of her hair. "I'll miss you too."

She let out a long sigh. "Can we make a deal?"

"What deal?"

"Can we not talk about you leaving? At least not until after Christmas. I just don't want... I don't want to think about it."

"That's a wonderful plan." He leaned down and kissed her gently. "Great plan."

He reluctantly pulled away and headed to his cottage. Violet did have a good plan. They wouldn't talk at all about his leaving.

The thing was, he couldn't stop his thoughts that easily. The fact he was leaving soon was always floating through his mind, taunting him, reminding him.

CHAPTER 27

Violet looked around the courtyard, smiling at the lights strung on the porch railings, winking at the fading daylight. She'd covered the table with a bright red tablecloth and carefully draped twinkle lights around the Christmas decorations on the table. Two silver lanterns adorned the table, casting a warm glow across the charcuterie trays and the spread of Christmas cookies she'd purchased from the cookie sale. A large red vase of bougainvillea with twinkle lights wound through its branches —she'd been very careful of the thorns— sparkled in the middle of the table.

Soft Christmas music filtered across the courtyard from a speaker she'd set up on the office porch. It all looked perfect, though she was sure Rob would say it was overkill.

Rose walked up and hugged her. "Look at this. What a magical place you've made the courtyard."

"Thank you. It's not too much?"

Rose laughed quietly. "No, never too much."

They both got a glass of wine, then Violet fiddled with the decorations on the table.

"I think George is stopping by tonight," Rose said.

"He is? Good. He can meet more people."

"I hope he's starting to feel more like he belongs here. Like he's part of Moonbeam."

"You're becoming part of the town, too. And I love that you're here for my first Christmas in Moonbeam. Sharing it with me."

"And I love that you're helping me through this first Christmas without Emmett," Rose said softly.

"To firsts." Violet raised her glass.

"To firsts. And making new memories," Rose said as she raised her glass and clinked it lightly against Violet's.

George came over and joined them as more of the guests filtered out of their cottages and came out for happy hour. She tried to keep from constantly looking over at Danny's cottage, waiting for him to show up.

"Hey, sis." Rob and Evelyn walked up to them. "The courtyard looks great. Love what you've done with the lights."

She eyed her brother. "You do?"

He laughed. "I do. As my favorite sister once said, you can never have too many Christmas decorations."

She didn't know why Rob's approval pleased her so much. She certainly didn't *need* it. But it was nice to hear the compliment.

"Looks great."

She whirled around at the sound of Danny's voice.

"Hi." She could only get the one word out as she stared at him. His hair was damp from a shower. A bright blue shirt stretched across his broad shoulders. But it was his eyes that captured her. They simmered with a stormy blue tempest. It was all she could do to keep from standing on tiptoe and kissing him right in front of everyone. How was it when Danny was around, the rest of the world just faded away?

"Danny, glad you're here. My sister, Donna, wanted to make sure that you got invited to our Christmas Eve gathering tomorrow."

Evelyn's words interrupted her thoughts, and she dragged her gaze from Danny's lips. Kind of.

"I don't want to crash your family time."

"Nonsense. We'd love for you to come. Emily will love having Allison there too." Evelyn turned to Rose and George. "And you two come, too. Please."

"I'd love to." Rose nodded.

"I appreciate the invitation," George said, his eyes twinkling with anticipation. "Thought I might be spending the holiday alone."

"We can't have that." Evelyn smiled at George.

Gratitude surged through Violet that Evelyn had included both Rose and George. And Danny. She was ridiculously happy that he and Allison would be there spending Christmas Eve with her.

Happy hour went longer than usual. It seemed like no one wanted the evening to end. At least she didn't want it to end. She wanted to spend more time with Danny.

As the last guests disappeared, Danny turned to her. "Finally. I've been wanting to kiss you all evening."

Exactly her thoughts.

He pulled her into his arms and kissed her. Then kissed her again.

"Really? Is that all you two do? Stand around kissing?"

She stepped back quickly at the sound of Allison's voice.

"And all you do is catch us kissing?" Danny teased his daughter.

"Well, if you're always kissing her, then it's not my fault if I keep interrupting." Allison laughed.

"Guess what. We got invited to the Parker get-together tomorrow night," Danny said.

Allison's eyes lit up. "We did? A real family Christmas Eve?" She clapped her hands. "I cannot wait." She twirled around. "Going to be the best Christmas ever."

Violet had to kind of agree with Allison's sentiment. It was turning into the best Christmas ever.

"I'm going to head in and finish my book. You two can go back to kissing." Allison grinned and headed over to their cottage.

"I love seeing her like this," Danny said as he watched his daughter leave. "She's so happy here." He turned back to her. "And I appreciate your family inviting us."

"They're not really my family. They're Robbie's family."

"I'm pretty sure they think of you as family too."

She shrugged. "Maybe. Kind of."

Danny took her hand. "I should probably go in. See if Allison wants some popcorn. We seem to have settled into a ritual of sharing popcorn or a snack at the end of our evenings here. I'm just so grateful that things are finally sorted out with us. I love having my daughter back. Best Christmas present I could ever have."

"I'm glad things worked out too."

He kissed her, then turned and walked back to his cottage. As he slipped inside, she reached up and touched her lips, swearing she could still feel the heat of his kiss on her lips. She was going to miss his kisses. Miss him.

But what was their promise? They wouldn't talk about him leaving until after the holidays. So she wouldn't think about it either.

Or at least she'd try not to.

CHAPTER 28

Danny was up early the next morning, excited for what the day had in store for them. The Christmas party at Donna's. And he had the perfect gift for Allison, all wrapped up and hidden in his room. He'd give it to her tonight before they left to go to Donna's.

Allison came hurrying out of her room before the coffee had even finished brewing.

"What are you doing up so early?"

"Shift at the cafe. They're only open until two this afternoon. They give all their employees the time off tonight and tomorrow."

"So you'll be back this afternoon?"

She nodded. "And then we'll go to the Parker's party tonight. I can't wait. I picked up a book on history that I'm giving to Emily."

"That was nice of you."

"What did you get for Violet?"

He frowned. He hadn't gotten her anything. What had he been thinking? Earlier, he'd debated if they were at the gift-giving stage. But now, of course, he needed a gift for her. It had been a long time since he'd bought a woman a gift. He had no clue.

"I guess I'm going shopping this morning."

"Really, Dad? You haven't gotten her anything yet?" She rolled her eyes at him but this time it was more in a teasing way than she was annoyed at him way.

"Any ideas?"

"You're on your own for this one. And you need to make sure it's a good gift. Something that means something."

He sighed. The pressure was on now. What in the world could he get that would be just the right thing?

"And, Dad, you should come by the cafe for breakfast this morning."

Well, that was a change. She wanted him to come to the cafe. "Okay, I'll be there in a bit."

"See you later." She rushed out of the cottage.

He poured himself a cup of coffee and sank

into a chair at the table. What in the world was he going to get Violet? And now he had to find it in town. There was no time to order anything online.

And he wanted the gift to be perfect. No pressure there...

Danny walked into the cafe an hour later, disappointed he still didn't have an idea for a gift for Violet. Guilt hammered him that he hadn't thought to buy her something before this. What kind of boyfriend was he?

Boyfriend? Was he her boyfriend? But what else would you call it? They dated. Hung out. Kissed. They kissed a lot.

He shook his head, clearing the jumbled thoughts from his mind.

Allison waved to him and pointed to a table by the window. He took a seat and she brought a menu and a glass of water. "Evelyn made cinnamon rolls."

He grinned. "Then you know what I'm having."

A tall, dark-haired young man came up to the table, his arms full of a tray of dishes he'd cleared. "Hey Allison, your customers over there need their check."

"Okay, thanks, Jake." She turned to him as the young man disappeared into the kitchen. "That's Jake. He works here. He's been away and just got back in town. Which is good, I guess, because they'll need him after I leave." She frowned. "I hate thinking about leaving."

"Me too, honey."

Allison hurried away, and he watched her chat with the nearby table of six and hand them their check. She hurried off to ring them up, returning with their credit card. Then she swung by a table and poured coffee, and stopped by another table to chat with them for a minute. When had she learned to handle all this? And to do it all so efficiently?

Jake came out and delivered his breakfast. "Mr. Parker, Allison asked me to bring this out to you. We're so busy this morning that we're helping each other out. I'm Jake, by the way."

"Nice to meet you, Jake."

"I just got back to town last night. Sounds like Allison has done a great job filling in for me while I was gone. Too bad she can't stay though. We could use the extra help."

Jake waved to a couple coming in the door. "Better go seat them." He hurried away.

Jake seemed like a nice young man. Friendly. Hard-working. There was a lot of that going around in the young people here in Moonbeam.

He ate his breakfast, still wracking his brain, trying to come up with a gift for Violet. He glanced out the window and the large container of flowers across the way caught his attention.

Then he knew exactly what he was going to get her.

CHAPTER 29

Allison came out of her room dressed in a light red sweater and slacks. Her eyes sparkled with excitement. "I'm so excited about going to this party. It feels like a real Christmas again this year, doesn't it?"

"It really does." He hugged her. "And how about I give you your Christmas present now?"

"Tonight?"

He laughed. "Yes, I can't wait any longer." He retrieved a small box wrapped in gold paper with a red ribbon from his room. Okay, it wasn't a great wrapping job, but he'd tried.

Allison slowly unwrapped the box and opened it. She gasped. "Oh, Dad. Gran's locket."

"I want you to have it. I've been carrying it

around since Mom died. Made me feel close to her."

"Are you sure?"

"I'm sure. I hope it does the same for you. Makes you feel her with you. She's always here, you know. In our hearts. In our memories."

Allison's eyes filled with tears. "I know she is. I can feel her sometimes. Will you help me put this on?"

He draped it around her neck and hooked the fastener. She turned around, fingering the delicate locket.

"I love this, Dad. You couldn't have picked out a better present for me."

"I'm glad you like it." The gold locket hung against her red sweater, and the image of Allison wearing the locket mingled with his memories of his mother wearing it. "It was your great-grandmother's locket, you know. She passed it on to Mom. I know Mom would want you to have it."

"I'll treasure it always." Allison swiped away a tear that rolled down her cheek.

He cleared his throat, chasing away the tears that threatened his own eyes. "We should get going."

She perked up. "We should. I can't wait."

"Oh, I picked up some flowers to bring to Donna for having us. I'll just grab them and we'll go."

Allison narrowed her eyes. "You didn't just get Violet a bouquet of flowers, did you? That's kind of weak."

He laughed. "Nope, I did better than that. Trust your old man."

Violet stood with Evelyn and Rob, anxiously waiting for Danny to show up. Donna had the whole point strung with white Christmas lights. Holiday music flowed around them. All the Parker family, plus numerous friends, stood around in small groups, laughing and talking. And yet, she still felt slightly like an outsider. But that was probably all in her mind. They were nothing but super welcoming to her.

She'd wanted to walk over with Danny and Allison, but Robbie had insisted she come with him and Evelyn. And how could she refuse her brother's family-should-be-together-on-Christmas guilt trip?

A wide grin spread across her face when she saw Danny and Allison walk in. Allison scurried off over to Emily and Blake, and Danny crossed over to her. "Hey." His smiled captured her gaze, and he reached out and took her hand.

She didn't miss that Robbie stared down at their clasped hands and a slight frown flashed before he covered it with a smile.

She flashed him a mind-your-own-business look.

Robbie stuck out his hand—whether he was just being friendly or trying to get Danny to drop her hand was anyone's guess.

Danny did drop her hand to shake Rob's. "Merry Christmas."

"I'm glad you and Allison could make it," Evelyn said, possibly unaware of the war going on between Robbie and her.

"I truly appreciate the invitation."

Robbie and Evelyn headed over to talk to Donna and she was finally alone—well, on a large patio with close to fifty people—with Danny.

"You look beautiful," Danny said as he took her hand again.

"You do too. Handsome I mean." He was drop-dead handsome in a blue shirt that brought out the sea-blue hue of his eyes.

Before she could enjoy more than a

moment, Emily and Allison came walking over. Then Rose and George. Soon any chance for alone time was gone, but she didn't really mind. She enjoyed being included in the gathering. Besides, tonight after all this was over, she hoped Danny would come to her place so she could give him his gift.

CHAPTER 30

Danny stood with Violet, chatting with all the people he'd come to know over the last few weeks. He smiled as he watched Allison chatter away with Emily, completely happy and content. He was so glad he was able to give this to her. A normal Christmas.

Emily stopped talking to Allison and turned and waved to an older lady walking out on the patio. "Grandmother. Come over here. I want you to meet some people."

The woman was dressed in stylish slacks and an evergreen sweater and glided across the distance, poised and collected.

"Hello, Emily, dear."

"Grandmother, this is Danny and Allison Parker. This is my great-grandmother, Patricia.

Patricia held out her hand. "So nice to meet you," she said politely.

He shook her hand, surprised at her firm grip.

"Funny that they're Parkers too. Isn't it?" Emily grinned.

"There are a lot of Parkers in this world, Emily."

"I'm working on some town research for a paper, and I got stuck a few generations back on Parkers. Let me run inside and grab some photos for you to look at. I have all these questions." Emily hurried off.

"Emily is quite the historian," Patricia said. "Always wanting to know more and more about the town and the Parkers."

"The history museum wants a copy of her paper when she finishes it," Allison piped up.

Emily returned with a stack of photographs. Patricia slipped on the reading glasses she had hanging on a chain around her neck and peered at the photos. A warm smile slipped across her face.

"Ah, yes. That's Grace Parker."

"I recognized her. And Mary Lou, her daughter. But who is that other boy?"

"That's L. My uncle. I never met him though. My mother rarely talked about him."

"Grace had two kids? I thought she just had your mom."

"No, she had a son. He got into some kind of trouble and left town. Headed west, I believe. The family never really talked about it. But my grandmother—Grace Parker—had a photograph of him on her bedside table."

"His name was L. Like the letter?" Emily frowned. "Was that a nickname?"

"I guess. It was just what my mom called him." Patricia frowned. "But I think if you go up to that storage room in the house, there's a box with some old things of Grace's in it. On the top shelf. In the back. Maybe you can find something more in there."

Emily raced off.

"I'm glad you could join our Christmas Eve gathering," Patricia said to them. "We go to midnight candlelight service at the church if you'd like to join us."

"Can we, Dad? Please?" Allison begged.

Not that it took any convincing. "Of course we can. That sounds nice." They used to go to the late candlelight service with his mother, but they skipped it last year.

Emily returned, her eyes shining. "Look what I found. It was wrapped in paper, tucked behind the box." She held up a weathered Bible.

"Oh. I haven't seen that in years." Patricia reached for it. She opened it to the first page. "Yes, here it is. Where the births, deaths, and marriages were recorded." She ran her finger down the page. "Grace had Mary Lou and... Elliot."

"So it's El, short for Elliot." Emily clapped her hands.

Danny frowned. "Elliot?"

"Yes, Elliot James Parker."

Danny's heart pounded. "Elliot," he repeated.

"Dad's middle name is Elliot." Allison stepped forward.

Patricia gasped, drawing everyone's attention. "Allison, where did you get that necklace?"

"From my dad. It's my Christmas present. It was my grandmother's. And her mother's."

"Open it, child," Patricia commanded.

Allison did as she was told and clicked the front cover open. He knew the photos they'd see. One of him. One of Allison.

"Slip out the photo on the right."

Allison peeled out the photo of her as a little girl.

Patricia stepped forward and fingered the locket, leaning close. "I can't believe it."

"What?" Emily asked, frowning.

"See that? Those initials. GP. Grace Parker. I've seen this locket in old photos of Grace. Her husband gave it to her and had her initials put in it. Mother told me about it but said Grace lost it. But she didn't. She must have given it to Elliot before he left Moonbeam."

Allison stood with her mouth open. He didn't fare much better. "You mean my mother's locket... was Grace's?"

Patricia nodded.

Emily let out a whoop. "You know what that means, don't you? We're family."

Stunned, he could only stand there, trying to take it all in.

"Mom, Evelyn, Heather, everyone. Come over here," Emily called out.

Soon they were surrounded by everyone as Emily retold the story and how they figured it all out.

Violet stood at his side, her hand on his arm, the only thing that was connecting him to reality right now. Grounding him while he processed

the news. They'd gone from a family of two...
to a family of who knows how many.

"You doing okay?" Violet leaned close and
whispered.

"I honestly don't know."

Allison came up and grasped his arm. "Oh,
my gosh. Dad. We're Parkers. We have a
family." Allison twirled around. "I'm a Parker
woman!"

Emily threw her arms around Allison, and
they laughed and spun around. As the news
sunk in, a wide smile spread across his face. He
had given Allison a great Christmas present.
Even better than the locket. He'd given her a
family for Christmas.

And then he thought of one more present
he could give her...

Late that night, after the candlelight service,
Violet stood with Danny on the porch of the
office. He'd gone into his cottage and come back
with two Christmas bags, grinning. "I got you a
little something."

He handed her the first bag. She peered

inside and pulled out a pretty teal pot full of dirt? She looked at him questioningly.

"It's an amaryllis bulb. It should bloom in about ten weeks, give or take. I thought when it bloomed... even after we're gone... that you'd think of me."

She gulped back tears. "We're not supposed to talk about you leaving. Not until after the holidays."

"You're right. I'm sorry," he said softly. "Here, open the next one."

She took the second bag and reached inside, pulling out a book. "Oh, a book on the flowers of Southern Florida. That's perfect. Thank you."

She handed him his present to open. He unwrapped it and smiled at her.

"It's Rob's newest book. And he signed it, too. I know you've been reading more now."

"Thank you. I can't wait to read it."

They stood awkwardly on the porch, holding their gifts. The amaryllis mocking them. Reminding them that he was leaving soon.

He leaned over and kissed her gently. "I might have one more present for you. But I need to figure something out first."

She frowned at his cryptic words. "You don't

need to give me anything else. These are lovely gifts."

He smiled, his face holding a hint of... excitement? "I've gotta go. I'll see you in the morning?" He turned and hurried across the courtyard.

"Merry Christmas," she whispered into the night.

CHAPTER 31

Danny was up early the next morning. He had tossed and turned during what little time he'd spent in bed, then finally gave up. The news that he and Allison had a family—a large family—was a bit overwhelming. Everything had turned upside down last night. He wished his mom was alive to hear the news, but somehow he felt like she knew.

Allison finally woke up, sleep still in her eyes as she stumbled into the kitchen. "Hope you saved me some coffee."

"Morning, sweetheart."

She poured a cup of coffee and sank onto the chair across from him. "Wow, that was quite a night, wasn't it? I can't believe Emily and I are related. She's going to figure out the exact relationship. She's good at stuff like that. But we decided we're just going to consider ourselves cousins."

"Good plan."

Allison glanced over at the tree and frowned. "What's all that? You already gave me my present."

"Just a few more things."

She went over and picked up the gifts, then returned to the table.

"Open them."

She opened up the first box and grinned. "More books by my favorite author. Oh, and the history of Moonbeam. I love it, Dad."

He laughed. "And I bought it before I even knew our ancestors were from here. Guess the universe was giving me a nudge."

"Or Gran." She grinned and reached for the next box.

"Open it," he urged.

She opened the small box and looked inside, picking up an old antique key. "That's your key that you've always had. You said it was from your grandfather's house."

"It was. Not that he ever locked the door."

"I don't get it. You want me to have it?"

"Well, it's more a symbol."

"A symbol of what?"

"Of… and only if you want to… a symbol of the key to our new home."

She frowned. "We just moved to that house in Tallahassee."

"But I thought it was time we had a home, not a house." He leaned forward and took her hands in his. "How would you feel about… about moving here to Moonbeam? Being around family?"

Her eyes flew open wide. "Really? We can stay?" She jumped up and twirled around, then tugged on his hands, pulling him to his feet before throwing herself in his arms.

He held her tight for a moment before she whirled away again, dancing with joy. "This is the best, best Christmas present ever."

He smiled at her. "I thought you might like it."

"We'll find the perfect house this time. One that feels like home. Oh, can we get one on the beach?"

"We'll see what we can find." But he'd give her any house she wanted.

She stopped twirling and looked at him. "So much changed, didn't it? And what if you hadn't given me the locket? We might never have known the truth."

"I think maybe that locket wasn't really a present from me. Maybe it was from your grandmother. For both of us."

Allison reached up and touched the locket hanging around her neck. "I think you're right." Then with a whoop, she twirled one more time. "I've got to go call Emily."

She got halfway down the hall and turned around. "And don't you have someone you need to go see?"

He grinned. "I sure do."

Violet sat out on the porch, enjoying a moment of peace and quiet. Though, when it was this quiet and no one needed her to do anything for them, it was hard to hide from her thoughts. The thoughts that Danny and Allison were leaving.

She mulled over the miraculous revelation last night that Danny and Allison were related to the Moonbeam Parkers. She hoped that meant they would come back and visit often. But did she really want a long-distance relationship? Wouldn't that be hard? She'd had one long-distance relationship in her life, back in college when her boyfriend had transferred to a different school. That relationship lasted one month after he transferred. He'd found a new girlfriend and moved on.

But they'd been kids then. Surely adults could figure something out. But what if Danny didn't want to do the long-distance thing? She'd ask him as soon as she saw him. She had to know.

Right then he stepped out onto this porch, saw her, and waved. He jogged across the distance.

"Danny, we need to talk."

He nodded. "We do."

"I'll go first." She stood up and walked over to him. "I need to know... I need to know if you want a long-distance relationship. If that's what you want."

He shook his head slowly. "No, that's not what I want. I'm sorry."

Her heart started to crumble. "Okay, I understand. They're hard and... well, I just thought I'd ask."

He grasped both of her hands in his. "I

don't want a long-distance relationship because…"

He let go of one of her hands and brushed back a lock of her hair. How she would miss that gesture when he left.

"Because… I'm not leaving."

Her heart gathered itself back together and thundered in her chest. "You're what? What did you say?"

"I talked to Allison this morning. We're staying here in Moonbeam. We have family here." He touched her cheek. "You're here."

"You're… you're going to live here in Moonbeam?"

"I am. I'm pretty sure Allison and Emily are already searching online for the perfect house for us."

"Here? In Moonbeam?" Maybe if she kept repeating it, it would sink in.

He pulled her into his arms, holding her close. "Here in Moonbeam. With you. There's nowhere I'd rather be."

And now, finally, in that very moment, she felt like she was where she belonged too. In Moonbeam. With Danny.

"And one more thing you should know." His gaze never left her face."

"What's that?"

"I love you, Violet."

Her heart flipped in her chest, soaring for the sky, and tears threatened to spill. "And I love you, Danny Parker."

Danny gave her that impossible-to-resist grin. "Well, since that's settled, I guess I better kiss you."

"I guess you should." And the world faded away as he held her close in his arms.

CHAPTER 32

"Tara, Mom, Dad, hurry up. We're going to be late." Walker stalked around the kitchen in his parents' home.

"We've got enough time." Tara rolled her eyes at him. "We need to be there at ten. It's only nine thirty. We could go over and back to the cottage three trips in that amount of time."

"I just want to make sure everything is perfect. She's going to be so surprised." He fingered the box in his pocket.

"Yes, after last night, I'll be glad to have this over. You acted so strange around her. She had to know something was up."

"I was nervous. I *am* nervous."

"She's going to be surprised, but it will be a

good surprise. A great one. And you talked to Willow?"

"I did. Everything is all set."

"Then stop pacing the floor and wearing out the carpet. Mom and Dad will be ready in a few minutes." She shook her head at him.

"I can't help it, sis. I'm so excited."

Tara shook her head, grinning. "And I'm happy for you. Now you just have to hope she says yes."

He whirled around and stared at his sister. "You think she might say no?"

Tara slapped his arm. "No, you goofball. She loves you. She's going to say yes."

Their mother came into the kitchen. "Are you two bickering?"

"No, ma'am," they said in unison.

"Good, because it's time to go. I can't wait to have Aspen be part of our family."

"If she says yes to him…" Tara teased as she walked out the door.

Aspen trudged over to the office the next morning. She hadn't been hungry for breakfast. Last night at the party at Jimmy's, Walker had acted so strange. He'd talked to just about everyone there except her. Tara and her parents had been kind of distant too. Maybe they all were regretting taking her in, treating her like family. She wasn't family, though. She knew that. All she had for family was Willow. And Willow wasn't here.

She pushed into the office and found Violet and Rose talking, a wide smile on Violet's face. "What's going on?"

"Violet just found out that Danny and Allison are staying in Moonbeam."

"And guess what?" Violet's eyes shone with excitement. "Danny and Allison are related to our Parkers. To Donna and Evelyn and all of them."

"No. Really?" She stood there, shocked. But at least someone had good news this Christmas. She shook her head, trying to dispel her pity party. She pasted on a smile and walked over to the reception desk. "That's great news. They'll have a big family then, won't they?"

"They will. And that's why they're going to move here. To be by family."

Rose smiled. "And I think the fact that Danny is smitten with Violet didn't hurt any."

"And that Allison has made friends here,"

Violet added and sighed. "It's all so perfect. I can't imagine a more special Christmas."

And that's what Aspen had thought too. That she'd have a perfect Christmas with family and Walker. But Willow had cancelled and Walker was just... distant. She certainly hadn't had the perfect Christmas she'd hoped for. In spite of her best intentions, a sadness settled over her, impossible to chase away.

Rose walked over to the door and peered outside. "Hey, Aspen. You should come see this."

"What?"

"Come see." Rose grinned at her.

She walked out from behind the desk and over to the door. Rose stepped aside and Aspen stepped out onto the deck and gasped. "Oh."

Willow rushed forward and threw her arms around her. "Surprise, sis. Merry Christmas."

She clung to her sister. "You're here."

Willow laughed and finally stepped back. "We're here. We got up early this morning to get here."

"But you were spending it with Derek's family."

"We did spend a few days before Christmas

and Christmas Eve. But they understood I needed to be with you today."

Aspen hugged her sister again before she felt someone tugging at her arm.

"Hey, Aunt Aspen. I'm here, too." Eli's shining face looked up at her.

She leaned down and hugged him. "Hi, Eli. I'm so glad you came."

"Mom said we're going to play on the beach and build sandcastles and go eat at this Jimmy guy's place."

She laughed. "We'll do all of that." She reached out and took Derek's outstretched hand. "Thanks for bringing them here."

"I was glad to. Couldn't have Willow missing her first Christmas with her sister."

Willow stepped back. "And there's someone else here to see you."

Aspen looked up, surprised to see Walker, Tara, and their parents standing at the end of the deck. Walker strode up to her.

"What are you doing here?" She looked up at him, no longer seeing that cloaked look in his eyes that she'd been seeing the last few weeks.

"I'm here to see you, of course."

She looked from Willow to Walker. "Did you know Willow was coming?"

"I might have." He smiled, his eyes twinkling at her.

"Well, it was a wonderful surprise."

"And I have one more Christmas present for you."

She eyed him. "What's that?"

She gasped as he sank to his knees, holding out a ring box in his hand.

"Aspen, I love you. I can't imagine spending my life without you. You've brought such joy into my life. Would you do me the honor of marrying me?"

"I…" And suddenly the tears came and no words would form.

He knelt there patiently, holding out the box, staring up at her face.

"Yes, yes, I'll marry you." Finally, the words escaped, and he jumped up and gathered her into his arms. Where she belonged. Where she felt safe and loved. He kissed her and slipped the ring on her finger.

His family circled around her, hugging her. His mom and Tara had tears in their eyes too.

When at last they backed away, Willow moved next to her, slipping an arm around her waist. "It's a pretty perfect Christmas, isn't it?"

"The best one ever."

She stood by her sister, her family, and the family she would soon marry into. And finally, after all these years, she belonged.

CHAPTER 33

Rose sat out on the beach, watching the sunset on her first Christmas without Emmett. It had been hard, different, but she'd made some wonderful memories over the last few days.

"Mind if I join you?" George's deep voice broke through her thoughts. "Or would you rather be alone?"

"No, please. Join me. The sky is putting on quite the performance tonight."

He dropped to the sand beside her. "Are you doing okay? The first holiday is the hardest."

"I am doing okay. I'm actually a bit surprised. But Violet made sure I stayed busy—I knew what she was doing—and invited me to so many activities with her. And it was very different than the quiet Christmases I spent with Emmett. This one was filled with activities and celebrations. It's hard to feel sad with so much love flowing around me."

"I'm glad you're doing okay."

"I am... but I have to admit, I'm glad to have the first Christmas without Emmett behind me. And that I did okay."

"You're a strong woman. I knew you'd be fine."

"It just... hurts." And there were the tears. The ones she'd been holding back all day.

He sat quietly by her side, letting her cry it out. When the tears finally ended, she looked up at the sky, bursting with color, with life. Stars twinkled above as the water rolled endlessly to shore, a constant companion now.

And just like that, she knew what she had to do. She'd sell her house and move to Moonbeam. Because Moonbeam was home to her now. Home to this next stage of life.

She smiled at George, keeping her decision to herself for now. A peace settled over her, and her friend the blue heron swooped down from the sky and landed at the water's edge, turning to stare at her for a moment before taking a few steps and soaring away, as if Emmett had come to tell her he agreed with her decision.

I hope you enjoyed this holiday story. And I know you're wondering where Rose's book is! Don't worry. I didn't leave her out. Check out Sea Glass from the Past for Rose's story and more of Aspen and Willow.

As always, I want you to know how much I appreciate you. I hope you found a sense of home and belonging as you read this series. Your emails, reviews, and warm wishes fill me with gratitude. You make this storytelling journey so rewarding.

With much love, Kay.

COMFORT CROSSING ~ THE SERIES

The Shop on Main - Book One

The Memory Box - Book Two

The Christmas Cottage - A Holiday Novella (Book 2.5)

The Letter - Book Three

The Christmas Scarf - A Holiday Novella (Book 3.5)

The Magnolia Cafe - Book Four

The Unexpected Wedding - Book Five

The Wedding in the Grove (crossover short story between series - Josephine and Paul from The Letter.)

LIGHTHOUSE POINT ~ THE SERIES

Wish Upon a Shell - Book One

Wedding on the Beach - Book Two

Love at the Lighthouse - Book Three

Cottage near the Point - Book Four

Return to the Island - Book Five

Bungalow by the Bay - Book Six

Christmas Comes to Lighthouse Point - Book Seven

CHARMING INN ~ Return to Lighthouse Point

One Simple Wish - Book One

Two of a Kind - Book Two

Three Little Things - Book Three

Four Short Weeks - Book Four

Five Years or So - Book Five

Six Hours Away - Book Six

Charming Christmas - Book Seven

SWEET RIVER ~ THE SERIES

A Dream to Believe in - Book One

A Memory to Cherish - Book Two

A Song to Remember - Book Three

A Time to Forgive - Book Four

A Summer of Secrets - Book Five

A Moment in the Moonlight - Book Six

MOONBEAM BAY ~ THE SERIES

The Parker Women - Book One

The Parker Cafe - Book Two

A Heather Parker Original - Book Three

The Parker Family Secret - Book Four

Grace Parker's Peach Pie - Book Five

The Perks of Being a Parker - Book Six

BLUE HERON COTTAGES ~ THE SERIES

Memories of the Beach - Book One

Walks along the Shore - Book Two

Bookshop near the Coast - Book Three

Restaurant on the Wharf - Book Four

Lilacs by the Sea - Book Five

Flower Shop on Magnolia - Book Six

Christmas by the Bay - Book Seven

Sea Glass from the Past - Book Eight

WIND CHIME BEACH ~ A stand-alone novel

INDIGO BAY ~

Sweet Days by the Bay - Kay's complete collection
of stories in the Indigo Bay series

ABOUT THE AUTHOR

Kay Correll is a USA Today bestselling author of sweet, heartwarming stories that are a cross between women's fiction and contemporary romance. She is known for her charming small towns, quirky townsfolk, and the enduring strong friendships between the women in her books.

Kay splits her time between the southwest coast of Florida and the Midwest of the U.S. and can often be found out and about with her camera, taking a myriad of photographs, often incorporating them into her book covers. When not lost in her writing or photography, she can be found spending time with her ever-supportive husband, knitting, or playing with her puppies - a cavalier who is too cute for his own good and a naughty but adorable Australian shepherd. Their five boys are all grown now and while she misses the rowdy boy-noise chaos, she is thoroughly enjoying her empty nest years.

Learn more about Kay and her books at kaycorrell.com

While you're there, sign up for her newsletter to hear about new releases, sales, and giveaways.

WHERE TO FIND ME:
My shop: shop.kaycorrell.com
My author website: kaycorrell.com
authorcontact@kaycorrell.com

Join my Facebook Reader Group. We have lots of fun and you'll hear about sales and new releases first!
www.facebook.com/groups/KayCorrell/

I love to hear from my readers. Feel free to contact me at authorcontact@kaycorrell.com

facebook.com/KayCorrellAuthor
instagram.com/kaycorrell
pinterest.com/kaycorrellauthor
amazon.com/author/kaycorrell
bookbub.com/authors/kay-correll

Made in the USA
Middletown, DE
11 December 2023